T0086353

DA
MAINTENANCE
MAN

DA MAINTENANCE MAN

JOHNQUES LUPOE

DA MAINTENANCE MAN

iUniverse books may be ordered through booksellers or by contacting:

iUniverse
1663 Liberty Drive
Bloomington, IN 47403
www.iuniverse.com
844-349-9409

Because of the dynamic nature of the Internet, any web addresses or links contained in this book may have changed since publication and may no longer be valid. The views expressed in this work are solely those of the author and do not necessarily reflect the views of the publisher, and the publisher hereby disclaims any responsibility for them.

Any people depicted in stock imagery provided by Getty Images are models, and such images are being used for illustrative purposes only.
Certain stock imagery © Getty Images.

ISBN: 978-1-6632-2047-9 (sc)
ISBN: 978-1-6632-2048-6 (e)

Library of Congress Control Number: 2021907680

Print information available on the last page.

iUniverse rev. date: 04/12/2021

PROLOGUE

Finally after ten years of doing time in the Georgia prison system, Quies has returned to the streets of Atlanta. Not having anyone that he could lean on; his mind is sat on getting some fast money. Just to hold him off until he gets a job. Not having a gun, he knows that his lick has to be extra sweet. Because he wasn't trying to get caught up again.

As he walked the streets of downtown, he spotted a man getting out of a taxi cab. Quies quickly makes his way over to the taxi. "Excuse me sir can I get a lift"

"Oh I'm sorry sir, I'm bout to take my break"

Quies gets an inch closer to the cab driver and hits him with a hay-maker that laid the driver out. He quickly looks around in the area,then goes in the cab driver's pockets. As he pulls out a small stack of money, he takes off running while he places the money in his pocket. Running into Five Points train station, he hops the riel and gets on the Southbound train.

Arriving at the airport Quies gets off the train and gets on the bus that would take him to Riverdale. Making the bus just in time, he walks to the back of the bus while it drives off. As he rides down Upper Riverdale Rd he pulls out his money to count. Then he pulls the cord to let him off at the first hotel on Tarrah Blvd. and checks in.

Quies knew that this money wouldn't last him long.But it would work good enough to get him on his feet, and to stay at the hotel for a week.

CHAPTER 1

"Good morning Atlanta! You are tuned into V-103 Morning Show. We are going to start off this morning off with a little Chris Brown "Hold You Down", followed by Nikki and Beyonce.

"Damn it's that time already", Quies though as he rolled over to cut off his alarm and to get out of bed. As he headed to the bathroom, Quies looked around at his hotel room and knew that he had to do better. Being locked up for all that time was a major setback. So he went and got all freshened up, then hit the door to start his job hunt.

Quies walked the streets going to every store and restaurant applying for a job, but it was not looking good for him.

Unfortunately nobody wanted to hire a convict. After all that walking, Quies was getting hungry, but he didn't know what he wanted to eat. He walked back down the street heading to his hotel. He came up to Sonny's BBQ. Quies looked at Sonny's sign and saw a now hiring sign, with a Sonny's Special right above it.

Queis hurried and went inside to place his order and to see about getting the job. Once the manager walked by, Quies politely stopped him and asked about the now hiring sign. The manager pointed to a table and told Quies that he would be there in a minute to talk to him. As he sat at the table, he went in his bag and pulled out his food. Once he started eating, the manager walked by the table and dropped off an application and told him to fill it out and he will be right back.

Quies quickly wiped his hands and filled out the application.

1

Just as he was finished, the manager came back to the table and told him that he would start tomorrow. Quies was so excited, that he never even asked how much he would be getting paid or what he would even be doing. Queis said, "Yes Sir", then grabbed his food and left the restaurant.

As he left the restaurant, he was feeling excellent that he found a job. Once Quies made it back to the hotel, he jumped in the shower and got comfortable. Not knowing what it was he was going to be doing, Quies knew that he had to get some rest. He jumped in bed and turned on the TV to his favorite show, before he knew it, he was off to sleep. At 9:00 a.m. the next morning, Quies woke up and got dressed for work.

As he left out his room he made sure that all of his lights were off, then he headed for work. As he walked down the street to Sonny's, he was thinking about what his job title would be and how many females would be working with him. As he arrived at his new job, he noticed there were no cars in the parking lot. So he began to walk around the restaurant just to see if anybody else was there. Before he could even get to the back of the building, a cop shows up.

"Damn, here we go again" Quies thinks to himself. "Freeze, don't move!!"

"Man I ain't even did shit, I'm just trying to go to work."

"Well why did we just get a call from here and somebody said that they had a potential break in?"

"Sir, I don't know, this is my first day at work." "Ok well let me get someone to the door."

Knock!Knock!Knock! "Hello Officer"

"Ma'am, this young man says that he works here?"

"No he don't, I have never seen him before." "Ok Sir, put your hands behind your back." "Hold up, ain't no way in the hell you're about to lock me up, you need to call your other manager Mr. Malcolm, that's the one who hired me and started me today"

"Ma'am, do you want to call to make sure he is telling the truth?"

"Yes, I will do that, just to be on the safe side" "Ok, well sir can you sit on the curb, until she gets back?"

"No, I'll stand, Quies replied. As the lady returned, she told the officer that everything checks out to be true.

"Ok, well y'all have a good day, and sorry bout the misunderstanding sir." "Yeah, you good".

"Ok, well let me apologize and introduce myself. My name is Ms. Amy or you can just call me Amy."

"My name is Quies"

"Well Quies, do you know what your job title is?"

"No, I don't but I would like to know, and I would like to get started in whatever it is" "Ok, well let's get started."

"You will start off in the Sonny's Suit."

"Ok, not trying to be funny, but what is the Sonny's Suit."

"Oh, you will have to put this cartoon outfit on and stand on the sidewalk." "Ok, how much will I get paid for this?"

"We will start you off at $7.00 an hour, but you move up to washing dishes within two hours" As Quies stood there looking at Amy as she walked off, he was thinking to himself, was it worth it? Then he began to put on the outfit and make his way out the side door. Once Quies made it outside and found a good spot to dance and do other crazy things to get customers to come in, his two hours were up. Ms. Amy was calling him in so he could begin to wash the dishes.

The 12 o'clock rush hour had started. Quies walks inside and takes off the suit and jumped straight on the pots and pans.Before he knew it, hours had passed and he was getting hungry. So he took a quick break to find Amy and see when he was gonna get a break. Before he could find Amy, she found him and told him that he could clock out for the day.

Quies clocked out and then went to get himself a plate and sat at the table by the window. Quies opened up his tray and went head first. As he ate his food, he heard a sexy voice saying, "Excuse me sir." But he was too hungry to even look up or to say anything at that point. But before he knew it, the lady had sat down with him.

"Excuse me sir, my name is Punkin and I would like to ask you a few questions". Quies amenity stopped eating and noticed a sexy redbone with long hair sitting across from him. He grabbed a napkin and wiped his hands and mouth.

"Excuse me Miss, but can I help you?" "Yes you can."

"Ok what do you need help with."

"Well I just got two quick questions for you." "Ok let me have them."

"Do you want to make some real money and a lot more than what you make here?" "Hell yeah, no offense, but yes I would."

"Ok well do you have your driver's license?" "Yea but I don't have a car at the time."

"It's ok, we will supply you with all that you will need, just show up at this address tomorrow" Punkin handed Quies a business card that said Paradise Maintenance Service. Quies sat at the table thinking how he was going to quit Sonny's, but still be able to come back if he ever needed too. Punkin left him sitting at the table,but before she could get all the way out of his sight Quies took off running after her. "Yo Punkin, wait up." Quies shouted as he ran after her. As Punkin turned around Quies was grabbing her by her hand to get her to stop.

"Yes Quies, how can I help you?"

"Aye, I need a ride home and I would like for you to explain more about this job." "Oh I will do that just this one time but, you better not let me down tomorrow."

As they left the parking lot, Punkin begins to explain that he will need some type of maintenance skills. As they rode down the street, she went into deeper details. Before they knew it, they were pulling up at the hotel. Quies got out of the car and walked back around to the driver side of the car and leaned down and asked Punkin for her number. She told him "Everything you need to know is on the card", and then she pulled off.

Quies walked to his room and saw all of his bags sitting outside the door. He ran to get his stuff, then headed to the front desk to see why they put him out. As soon as he walked in the office, the lady at the front desk started yelling at him about paying his rent. Knowing that he just started working, he wouldn't have that check until next week. Quies had no family to turn to, so his only chance was to call Punkin and tell her what's going on. Hoping that she would help him out, Quies went to go use the phone in the lobby.

"Hello"

"Umm, may I speak to Punkin?" "This is she, how may I help you?"

"Hey this is Quies, I know you are going to be mad a me, but as of right now you're all I have." "Umm Quies what are you talking about?"

"I just got put out of my hotel room and I need somewhere to stay until I get my first check" "Oh no baby, I can't do that, I just met you." "Look Punkin, I promise I won't try anything and I will make you look good at work tomorrow."

"Damn it Quies, I'm only doing this because I see you are trying to help yourself, and I know your situation."

"Thanks a lot, I'll be at the entrance waiting for you."

An hour and forty minutes later, they arrive at Punkin's house.

"Ok Quies, you can sleep here in the guest room and your bathroom is right across the hall. If you need anything my room is down the hall to the left and here is a towel set for you to wash and dry off with."

"Ok, thanks"Quies replied. As he put his stuff down in the room and got ready to take a shower, it dawned on him why Punkin doesn't have a man as beautiful as she is. Quies went to take his shower and the whole time he was washing, he was thinking if he should try to make a move on Punkin.

Once he finished washing, he grabbed his towel and wrapped it around his waist. He walked out of the bathroom, as soon as he took his first two steps he bumped into Punkin.

"Oh, I am so sorry Punkin, I was just trying to run back to the room before you saw me." "Umm ... Umm ... It's ok, but you need to cover that little bird chest up."

Quies laughed and walked into the room. He noticed that Punkin couldn't take her eyes off of his body. As he got himself together, he heard some talking coming from the next room over. He decided to listen in to see who she was talking to and about what.

"Shun, let me tell you, his body is impressive, you wouldn't even think he had a body like this." "Umm...well do you think his sex game will match that body and looks?"

"Girl it's hard to tell, and you know I can't break the number one rule"

"Yea, you are right Punkin, but I'm ready to see him now, oh yeah did you tell him what he would be doing at work?"

"Yea somewhat, but I ain't told him everything. I'm pretty sure he won't mind it, hell what man would?"

"Ok Punkin, I guess I'll see y'all tomorrow" "Bye girl."

Quies began to wonder exactly what it was that he would be doing tomorrow. So he came out of his room and called for Punkin. "Aye Punkin, can you come here for a moment?"

"Yea sure thing, I'll be there in one second."

As Punkin walked down the hall putting her hair in a ponytail. Quies forgot what it was that he wanted to talk about. Being locked up for so long around nothing but men and fat chicks, this situation threw him off. It was hard to believe that he was now staying with a chick that could be a model.

"Yo Quies whats up?"

"Umm ... Umm .. can I use your phone to call and quit that other job?" "Yea sure, here you go."

Quies makes his call to handle his business, but he still didn't ask her what it was that he would be doing tomorrow. As he handed her the phone back, they made eye contact, but Punkin quickly broke it and ran back to her room. "Damn, I didn't know her ass was that fat", Quies thought to himself as Punkin ran back down the hall. Quies went and laid down to get some rest for tomorrow, but had a hard time due to many thoughts running through his head. The anticipation was killing him not knowing what Punking had planned for him, so Quies rolled around in his bed until he fell asleep.

The next morning, Quies got up and got himself together and ready for work. He had noticed that Punkin was just getting up. Quies went back to the room and sat on the bed. Thirty minutes later, Punkin comes walking into the room, but she sees that Quies is already up and ready. She gave him the keys to the car to go warm it up. Quies waited for her in the car.

As he sits there Punkin comes out of the house like she is ripping the runway. When she gets in the car she asks Quies what he wants for breakfast. He looked at her and told her it didn't matter, so Punkin looked at Quies and told him that they were going to her favorite spot. As they pulled up at the drive thru window, a voice came over the intercom, "Welcome to Chick-A-Fila, how may I help you?"

"Umm, yes can I have three chicken biscuits and two orange juices please?" "Will that be all ma'am?"

"Yes, that will be it."

"Drive up to the next window please."

Once they received their food, they headed to work. Quies realized how down to earth Punkin was. That made it even harder for him to make a move, not wanting to mess up anything between them. He told himself that he would just wait until the time was right. Before he knew it, they were pulling up at a small building. Punkin parked the car and told Quies to come with her.

As they got out of the car Quies couldn't help but notice that it wasn't nothing but women coming in and out of the building. He began to like his job already.

"Hey Shun, this is Quies the guy I was telling you about."

"Hello Queis, my name is Shun and I'm the owner of Paradise Maintenance Service." "Hi Shun."

"Well hopefully Punkin filled you in on everything?" "Yea but no", Quies said.

"Ok, well we are a maintenance company and we do just that, if you know what I mean?" "Ok, I think I follow, but I'm not sure."

"Well we will just let you work around here for a few hours until you get up to speed." "Ok, that's cool with me."

As the day went on Quies learned all kinds of new skills to put with his own. And watched nothing but women come in and out of the building. Quies didn't think anything of it, he just thought it was a lot of single ladies out there that needed help. He overheard one of the ladies ask about him and Shun pointed his way and said tomorrow. After the customer left Quies walked up to Shun and asked her what was that about.

She just looked at him and smiled, then told him he will be going out on his first job tomorrow. Now by this time it was a little bit after one o'clock and Quies hadn't eaten anything. But before he could even come from the back Punkin and Shun was calling for him. As he walked up front, he smelled some food. Walking into the break room he saw two large pizzas with a 2 liter of cola, he quickly washed his hands and started eating.

Shun and Punkin stood back and ate their slices of pizzas while they watched Quies. Quies paid them no mind as he ate, but he kept hearing them laughing and having their girl talk. After Quies finished eating, Shun told him to go and make sure that the van he will be using is full of gas. Quies headed outside to the cage to find his van. Once he found his van, he took it to get washed and cleaned out. As he filled up the tank a red Mercedes pulled up and a dark chocolate chick with long silky hair and hazel eyes was inside.

As she stepped out of the car, Quies got a better view of her.

Looking at her body made him feel some type of way. He wanted to kick himself in the ass cause she looked like she just ate an all you can eat buffet and still wanted more. Quies quickly jumped in the van and headed to the shop. Thinking to himself about how he almost went out bad.

He couldn't do anything but laugh to himself. Pulling back up at the shop, Quies didn't realize that the time had went by so quickly. Punkin was already in the car waiting for him. "Quies, just park the van, I already clocked you out", Punkin yelled out the window.

He parked the van, then walked to the car and got in. On the way home, Punkin informed Quies that, "All customers are not going to be the same, some you will have to work on and some of them, you are the work."

"Hold up Punkin, what do you mean, I am the work?"

"You will see what I am talking about tomorrow, it's nothing bad Quies."

Pulling up to the house, Quies couldn't wait to go take a shower and get ready for the next day. Quies couldn't stop thinking about work, he knew Shun and Punkin were hiding something, but it couldn't be bad cause they get a lot of business.

CHAPTER 2

The next morning Punkin came to wake Quies up, but he wasn't even in the room. Quies was already up and ready to go. Punkin couldn't do nothing but smile and grab her keys. Forty five minutes later they were pulling up at the shop. And this was Quies first time seeing all of the other employees. He figured he'd ask around to see what the big secret was with his job, but everyone told him the same thing, "All customers are not the same".

Quies just couldn't believe that nobody would tell him the big secret. So he went to his van, Punkin came up to him with a little brown bag and said don't let me down. He just looked at her and said ok as he jumped into the van. As he started the van up, he looked over his paperwork to see where he was going. He was familiar with the Roswell area, so he headed out.

An hour later, he arrived at his location. Pulling up in the driveway he noticed a lady out in the yard with a small dog. He parked the van and grabbed his clipboard and walked to the door. As he reached the door the lady was coming up behind him.

"Good morning Sir, right this way."

"Good morning Ma'am, how are you doing?" "I'm good, but not as good as I want to be." "What do you mean by that? If you don't mind me asking."

"You do know what you are here for right?" "Yea to fix your problem with the drain." "Well, if that's what you want to call it, then ok." The lady laughs as she walks into the bedroom. "Oh yea, my name is Nicki by the way, what's yours?"

11

"Quies! Ma'am."

"Well Quies, are you ready?"

"Yeah I guess, so where is the problem at?"

Before he knew it, Nicki dropped her robe then leaped into his arm. Kissing all over him until he fell back on the bed. Trying to stop her was a hard thing to do, cause the soft kisses were feeling so good. Quies didn't know if he should stop her for real or to go along with it since it's been awhile for him and Nicki wasn't making it any easier for him either.

Nicki had unfastened his belt and pulled his pants down just enough so she could begin to suck on him. "Hold up Nicki let me make it easier for you" Quies stood up and got butt naked and then took control. And laid Nicki on the bed and began kissing her all over and sucking on her breasts. He began working his way down low to lick and suck her kitty. Not even two minutes had passed and Nicki was cumming.

Quies came up and slowly placed himself inside of her. Taking it slow, feeling all of her juices and the tightness of her pussy. Quies began to speed up and go harder. The harder he went the tighter Nicki squeezed and moaned. Quies pulled out and flipped Nicki over to hit it from the back.

With each stroke he grabbed her ass and gave it a little smack. He began to lift Nicki up from the back in an upright position, giving her some long hard strokes. The faster he went, the more wetter she got until they both reached their climax. Then, Quies laid Nicki back on the bed and asked for a rag to clean up with. Nicki tried to stand up and walk but she was too weak.

So she sat back down and told him everything was in the bathroom. Quies went to go clean up and once he came back, Nicki was fast asleep. Queis decided to leave, so he left her laying on the bed and locked the door behind him. As he got into the van he called the shop to see where his next job was.

"Hello, Paradise Maintenance Service, this is Shun speaking, how may I help you?" "Hey Shun this is Quies, I was calling to see if you had another job for me?"

"Umm ... let me check. Ok, we have one on South Cobb Parkway. The address is 123 South Cobb Parkway."

"Ok I'm headed there now."

While heading to his next job, Quies couldn't stop thinking about the job he just left from. He didn't know if Nicki was going to call in on him because he didn't fix anything. But at the same time she didn't show him the problem. Quies was just going to have to wait it out. Pulling up at the location, Quies looked at the building to make sure he was at the right spot. As he walked inside, he was greeted by the receptionist.

"Hello, Welcome to Wet-N-Tights Workout gym."

"Hi, I'm here from Paradise Maintenance Service, we have an order about a leak." "Oh, right this way sir."

Following behind the greeter, Quies was amazed by her amazing shape in them tights, but he had to keep it all business because he didn't know if he was being tested.

"Right here sir, it's the third toilet." "Ok ma'am, I'll take care of it.

Meanwhile back at the shop, Punkin received a call from Nicki. Nicki was explaining everything to her, letting her know that she was well satisfied. And that is the best service that she's had. As Punkin hung up the phone, she started to log in the info in the customer service book. Then Punkin left the desk to find Shun and let her know how pleased Ms.Nicki was with Quies.

Punkin was curious if they should try Quies out with one of their wild customers. To see if he could handle it, but Shun wasn't ready to put him out there yet. She wanted to give him a few more test runs. As Punkin walked back to the receptionists desk, the phone was ringing.

"Hello, thanks for calling Paradise Maintenance Service, how may I help you?" "Hi my name is Kimberly and I was trying to get the Maintenance Man Special."

"Ok Ms. Kimberly, I can help you with that, I just need to get the following information from you and I'll send the first maintenance man available."

Before Punkin could get all of the info, Quies was calling in on the other line. "Ms. Kimberly can you please hold?"

"Yes " "Hello"

"Hey I just finished that last job, do you have anything else?"

"Yea, actually I got you one right here. It's a special so you should know it's like your first job. Here is the address, 4569 Buckhead Lane, her name is Ms. Kimberly."

"Ok, but Punkin when I get off I need to talk to you."

"Ok we will talk, but I have to go because I still got that customer on the other line."

Quies hung up the phone and put the address into the van's GPS system. As he headed to his next designation, it dawned on him that he was an undercover gigolo. Quies really liked the whole idea of this, but what he didn't know is if it would mess up his chances with Punkin. Or if he ever had one because he never said anything to her. He actually didn't know if he wanted to bring it up to her attention.

As Quies drove, he heard one of his favorite songs, "Southside" by Lil baby. That song brought back a lot of memories of when he was locked up. Quies turned up the radio and speeded down the highway. Five minutes later, he was coming up on his exit.

Quies got off the highway and made two lefts and a right, and he was in front of a big white house.

As he slowly pulled in the driveway, he double-checked to make sure it was the right address. Once he parked the van, he walked to the front door and knocked. A red headed white chick opened the door.

"Hello, you must be Quies?" "Yes I am ma'am."

"Well Quies I hope that you're ready for a little fun today?" "Yes ma'am, I am!"

"Ok just call me Kim."

They went to the room and Kim locked the door behind them. Kim told Quies to get comfortable as she went to the bathroom to freshen up. Quies started making himself comfortable, but before he could even get out of his pants, Kim came bursting out of the bathroom. She was dressed in an all black catsuit with a whip in one hand and some handcuffs in the other. Quies eyes grew bigger than two fifty cent pieces, He knew he had to get outta there.

Jumping off the bed running for the door, Quies tripped over his pants and fell on the floor. Kim quickly ran over and put the handcuffs on Quies. She then leaned him on the bed and rolled him until he was completely on the bed. Once she got him in the bed, she pulled out more cuffs and cuffed him to the bed. Quies was trying to move around but it was like Kim had turned in the SHE HULK.

Quies laid on the bed thinking to himself about how all of his working out didn't pay off. But at the same time it surprised him, because he was getting turned on. Kim stood on the side of the bed and began to pour oil all over Quies' body. Once she rubbed it in, she got her whip and started whipping him softly. Quies started yelling, but it slowly became a soft moan.

Kim noticed the print in his boxers had gotten bigger. She then came out of her catsuit and straddled him with her ass in his face. And pulled his boxers down and started jacking him, as she sucked and licked all over his cock. Then she reached around him and slowly rubbed on her clit. As her juices started flowing, the faster she got giving Quies head. "Yo Kim I got it, you don't have to do this on your own, just uncuff me." "Promise me that you won't run!"

"Trust me, I ain't going anywhere!"

Kim uncuffed Quies, then straddled him to finish what she started. But only this time Quies gripped Kim by her hips and went face first. He began sucking on her clit and tongue fucking her. Kim got wetter and wetter and she started squirting cum all into Quies mouth. Quies got up and laid Kim on the edge of the bed with both legs placed together in the air.

Quies then slowly slid himself inside of her. Taking deep hard strokes, Kim started to grasp him tighter and tighter. The faster and harder he went the louder Kim moaned. Quies then flipped Kim over and she got on all fours, he began to pound her from the back. As he stroked her from the back, he leaned over and got her toy off the nightstand and slowly slid it into her ass.

While pounding her from the back, Quies was sliding her vibrator in and out of her ass until she began cumming down her legs. Quies stood over Kim in a frog like position and went into hyper drive. Kim started biting on the pillow and moaned louder than she ever had before. With the vibrator still in her ass and Quies pounding her from behind. It became too much for Kim to handle. And she slowly started to fall forward as Quies continued to pound her as hard as he could.

Before he knew it, she had stretched out across the bed. Quies quickly rolled over and put Kim back on top. She suddenly jerked her hips in an up and down motion, and pulled out the vibrator from her ass. Then moved faster as she worked her kitty muscle. She had some more tricks up her sleeve, but all of a sudden Quies started yelling out "I'm Cumming!"

Kim jumped off of him and rapidly removed the condom and started sucking on him. Within seconds of her mouth begin all over his shaft, Quies released himself all in her mouth and on her face. Kim tried to get up, but her legs gave out. She laid back on the bed and looked at Quies with a Damn good look on her face. Quies got up smiling as he walked to the bathroom to clean himself up.

Once he got done,he walked back into the bedroom.Kim was posted up on the side of the bed asking for round two. As bad as he wanted to, he knew he couldn't. It was getting late and had to head back to the shop. As he walked out of the room, Kim started yelling and crying for him not to leave.

Quies didn't even look back, he just kept going. When he got close to the front door he heard footsteps coming towards him. He turned around to see Kim running after him with her whip and handcuffs. Quies grabbed his keys and ran out the door to the van. He jumped in and started the van up, Kim was still running towards the van with no clothes on.

Quies pulled out the driveway and didn't look back. As he drove down the highway, he made his call back to the shop, but nobody picked up. Quies checked the clock to see what time it was, it was only 4:30 and he knew that the shop closed at 5:00 pm. He then called Shun on her cell.

"This is Shun, may I help you?"

"Hey Shun this is Quies, I am on my way back to the shop unless you have another job for me?"

"Umm ... well we have a few more little jobs, but you can do them tomorrow." "Ok, can you tell Punkin I'll be there in 30 minutes or less."

"Ok we will see you when you get here."

As he hung up the phone, his stomach started growling. Working all day without anything to eat, Quies was hungry. He knew he had to talk to Punkin into cooking, or he would have to stop and get something to eat. He rushed down the expressway to get back to the shop. Pulling up at the shop, he saw Shun and Punkin locking the doors.

He drove to the back of the building and parked the van. As he locked the doors on the van, Punkin was pulling up for him to get in the car.

"Hey Quies, I got you something to eat from Checker's, I hope that's cool?"

"Yea, that's cool cause I am hungry as hell." "Ok cause I know you didn't take any break today. Oh yeah, what is it that you wanted to talk about?"

"Oh yeah! Ummm I didn't know how to tell you."

"Well, while you are trying to figure out what you want to say, I have a few more questions myself."

As they drove home, they asked all the questions that they had. Once they made it to the house, Quies got his things and went straight to the shower. The whole time he was in the shower he was thinking about Punkin. And what was on her mind since he told her that he was feeling her, because she really didn't say much about the topic. In the meantime, he just finished showering.

He went to his room to get dressed. As soon as he got dressed, he laid across the bed and turned the TV on. Quies was looking for something to watch but he fell fast asleep. Punkin peeked in the room to talk to him but she saw him knocked out. She just pulled the door shut and went back to her room.

At this point Punkin had some questions to ask Quies, but she couldn't. She then went back to her room to reverie and think to herself. Laying on her king size bed with the pillowtop, Punkin went right to sleep.

CHAPTER 3

Bang!!'Bang! ! Bang!! Quies jumped out of bed and looked around to see where the banging was coming from. Walking out of the room, Punkin shot right by him at top speed. Quies jumped back because she had scared him. He came back out of the room and the banging got louder. As he walked to Punkin's room he saw her sitting in the corner with all her lights off.

"Yo Punkin, what's going on?"

"Quies, please go back to your room."

"Why, what's wrong? Who and the hell is that anyway beating on the door like that?" "It's my ex-boyfriend, he is crazy and he wants me to take him back."

"So what's up, you want me to handle this, it's too early in the morning for this shit." "No, cause he has a gun he wants to kill me if I am with someone else."

"Damn girl, that kitty must be fire."

"Quies, this ain't no time to be joking, just go lay back down, he will leave in a minute." "Ok, if that's what you want. I'll see you in a few hours."

Quies walked back to his room laid back down. It didn't take long for him to fall back asleep. The banging had stopped and it was quiet as a burial site. Time had flown by, Quies was now waking up to the sound of his alarm. As he got up, he noticed that Punkin had slept with him for those two hours.

He tapped Punkin on her shoulder to wake her up, then he got ready for work. Once he was ready, Quies took a walk around to make sure that her ex was gone. Not seeing anybody or no cars out front made Quies have a funny feeling. Because he knew that normally there would be at least two or three people warming their cars up.

Quies went back in the house to see if Punkin was ready.

As he was coming down the hallway, Punkin was coming up. He turned around and they left out the house. Getting in the car, Quies looked at Punkin and saw that she was still scared. Heading to work, he asked her what was up with her and that dude. At this point, Punkin was afraid to even talk about the whole situation.

As she looked at Quies, he could tell that she wanted to ask for help, but just didn't know how. Arriving at the shop, Quies spotted a blue Monte Carlo slowing down as they drove by and then speeding up once they got out the car. He didn't say anything to Punkin, he just walked inside the shop to get his work load for the day. Before he could even walk away, Shun pulled him over to tell him to keep up the good work and that all of his customers have given a good report on him.

Quies smiled and walked off. As he got in his van, he let it warm up as he punched in the address into his GPS. Leaving out of the parking lot, he noticed Monte Carlo sitting in an empty lot a block down from the shop. As he got on the expressway he texted Punkin and told her to be careful. Driving down the highway, Quies saw a blue car weaving in and out of traffic, but he wasn't sure if it was the Monte Carlo or not.

Quies kept an eye out for the car as he made his way down the highway. Getting off his exit he didn't see the car anymore, so he just headed to his job site. As he arrived at his location, he stopped to look around to make sure he wasn't being followed. Quies knocked on the door and while he was waiting, he heard a car driving by. Quies quickly turned around to make sure it wasn't the Monte Carlo and at the same time the front door opened up. When the door opened

Quies turned around with a startled look on his face. "Hey sir, are you ok?"

"Yes ma'am, I am. My name is Quies and I'm from Paradise Maintenance Service, how are you today?"

"Oh ok, I'm good and right this way Mr. Quies."

Quies followed the lady down stairs to the basement into a little room that was like a utility room. As she showed him what the problem was, he couldn't help but stand there looking at her body and staring at her lips. Quies was hypnotic about her small, but thick frame. She was no taller than 5'3, with long silky black hair and hazel-green eyes and a caramel complexion. She couldn't have weighed no more than 135 pounds. When Quies came out of his daze, the lady was just looking at him and laughing.

"Excuse me ma'am, what was your name again?" "It's Sanaa like the actress."

"Oh ok, well Ms. Sanaa I'll go ahead and take care of this for you." "Are you sure, cause for I second I thought lost you."

"Real cute, but honestly I was just checking you out."

"Oh yeah, so do you like what you see?" "You're alright." "Well, since I'm just alright, I'll let you get back to work."

As Sanaa walked off, Quies couldn't help but watch her walk away. As she walked off, it was like she was throwing her hips harder and harder to make her ass bounce even more because she knew he was looking. Once she went back upstairs, Quies quickly started repairing her leaking pipe. It took him almost an hour to finish, and to get everything cleaned up. He made his way back upstairs to see Sanaa sitting on the couch watching CNN.

He then walked up to her to let her know that he was finished. And to also find out what was happening on the news. Sanaa turned around and started explaining what was happening in New York. The police just jumped on another black guy. "Damn, that sucks." Quies replied while shaking his head, and then told her to have a nice day as he left out the door.

Before he could even turn back around to say anything else to her, she was standing in the door with a business card. After he took the card she was winking her eye at Quies, but he just smiled with her card in hand and walked off. Getting into the van, he grabbed his next job form and put the address in the GPS. As he hit the road his phone went off.

"Hello!"

"Hey Quies, this is Shun."

"Oh, what's up, I thought you were Punkin."

"No, but that's why I'm calling, have you heard from her?"

"No, not since this morning, but I did send her a text and told her to be careful." "Why did you do that, what's wrong?"

"Well, this morning her ex came beating on the door and when we got to work, I saw a blue Monte Carlo drive by real slow."

"Dam that crazy nigga is back at it again. Let me see if I can track her down" "Ok well tell her to call me ASAP when you find her."

"Ok I will."

Pulling up at a small building, Quies parked on the side and walked inside. While waiting for the receptionist to come out, he called Punkin just to see if she would pick up, but before he could leave a message the receptionist popped up.

"Hello sir, welcome to Whacky Weave's Hair Salon, my name is Alexis how may I help you?"

"Hi Alexis, my name is Quies and I'm here from Paradise Maintenance Service to fix a pipe line or something to that nature."

"Oh yes, right this way sir."

Alexis showed him where he would be working. Once he saw the problem he knew he would be there for a minute. He went back to the van to get all of his tools that he would need. Quies started breaking up the concrete to get to the pipes. Five hours later, Alexis came back to check on Quies and to bring him some lunch.

He was now cleaning up the mess that he had made. Alexis began to check out his work to see how good of a job he did. While Alexis was looking over his work, Quies took his tools back to his van. When he returned to the building Alexis was at the front desk with his lunch.

"Thanks for the lunch."

"Well you've earned it, you've been working hard."

"Well thanks, that's my job. I have to make sure the problem gets fixed and the customer is happy."

"Well I am very happy, now I can open my salon back up." "Thanks again for lunch, unfortunately I have to eat and run."

Quies made sure everything was in the van so he could head to his next job. On his way to his next job, his phone began to ring. "Hello."

"Hey Quies, this is Punkin. Shun told me that you called looking for me."

"Yea I did, I just wanted to check on you and make sure you were ok. Because Shun called me looking for you."

"Oh yea she told me she called you but, I just had to run and

24

take care of a few things." "Ok, well I'm glad to know that you are ok. I'll see you when I get back to the shop."

"Ok Boo ... I mean Quies."

Quies got off the phone because he had passed by the house. Turning into the next driveway to turn around, he saw his customer pulling up. He felt good cause he was right on time. So he hurried and pulled up in the driveway. As he got out of the van he saw the garage shutting, so he just went to the front door.

He began knocking on the door, as he spotted a tall lanky white dude coming to the door. The door opened and the guy was standing in the doorway with a nursing uniform on.

"How may I help you?"

"I'm here from Paradise Maintenance Service and I see that you requested the Maintenance Man Special, but I'm sorry to tell you sir, I don't do men."

"Oh no, it's not for me it's for my wife I'm just going to watch." "For your wife! And are you sure about this sir?"

"Yes I am and I would like for you to really give it to her too."

"Well if that's what you want then ok, you are the paying customer." "Great, my name is Billy and my wife is Lira."

When they made it up to the room, Lira was already half naked coming out of the shower. Quies looked at her then looked at Billy, he could see why Billy had called for help. Billy's wife looked like she could have been part of the Kardashian family. Quies didn't waste any time getting undressed. As soon as he was naked, Lira got on her knees and started serving him.

Quies got an erection in no time. As she was sucking and licking on Quies, he peeked to see what her husband was doing. Once he saw him sitting in the chair, he got comfortable. Quies then pulled

Lira off her knees and bent her over the bed. Slowly sliding himself inside of her. Quies could see that she ain't never really had no dick, before so he knew this would be fun to beat it up.

Quies started taking long deep strokes as he grabbed her ass. The harder he got, the louder she screamed. Quies thought back to what her husband had told him, about giving it to her hard and rough. He began pulling her hair and smacking her ass. Then he flipped her over on her side with one leg in the air and started stroking her at an angle.

Lira squirmed up the bed trying to get away. Quies dragged her back down to him and went in her even harder. He picked her up and started bouncing her up and down on him. Then he walked over to the other end of the bed, while he was still pumping her . He then laid her on the end of the bed, on her back and put her legs behind her head.

Quies put one of his legs next to her body, then leaned forward and bounced up and down inside of her making her climax. Quies then laid on top of her with her legs still up, he then began humping her hard and fast, then going slow to fast again. Lira wrapped her arms around his neck and squeezed as tight as she could. Biting her bottom lip and looking at Quies with those pretty brown eyes. That turned him on even more.

He started going even faster. Reaching his climax, he pulled out and ejaculated all over her. Billy stood up and started clapping and thanking him for the good performance. Quies grabbed a pillow and covered himself up cause he had forgotten that Billy was still in the room. Quies quickly went to the bathroom and cleaned up.

As he was coming out of the bathroom, he saw Billy on his knees giving Lira oral sex. He shook his head and started heading for the front door. Before he got to the door, he turned around and took one last look at Lira. Lira had the look on her face, which indicated that she didn't want Quies to leave. And also that she wasn't really into what Billy was doing, but Quies knew he couldn't stay any longer.

Getting into the van, he saw that he had 10 missed calls. As he started the van he checked his phone and all of the calls had come from his job. Driving off, he called the job to see what was wrong.

"Hello, hi thanks for calling ..."

"Hey sorry to cut you off but, who is this, Punkin or Shun?" "This is Punkin, who is this?"

"This Quies, I was calling cause I had ten missed calls." "Umm ... I forgot what I wanted but, where are you?" "I'm on the way back to the shop, it's about that time." "ok well hurry up cause I'm ready to go"

"Ok, I'll be there in a few minutes. You know this last job wasn't too far from the shop,so I'll be there in a few."

"Ok I'll be waiting."

As they hung up the phone, Quies thought that it was unusual for Punkin to call him like that. Quies just speeded up so he could get back to the shop. Once he got back to the shop, he hurried and parked the van then went inside. As soon as Punkin saw him she ran and gave him a big hug. She then looked at him and said, "nigga lets go."

He laughed at her as he walked off. As soon as they got in the car, Punkin started talking about her day. Quies could tell that Punkin had become more comfortable with him. The whole ride home Quies was thinking about how he had grown on Punkin, and now was the perfect time for him to make his move. Coming up to the house, Punkin thought she had seen her ex-boyfriend.

So she drove by the house and made sure it wasn't him. By the time she got back to where the guy was standing, he was gone. She turned around and went straight to the house pulling her car in the garage, so no one would know she was home. While Punkin was getting her stuff out of the car, Quies went inside to take a shower. Punkin came in and made herself comfortable and started to cook dinner.

She heard her phone ring so she took off running down the hall. Before she could even make it down the hall, she got knocked over by Quies coming out of the shower. Punkin was sitting on the floor in a daze, she couldn't take her eyes off of Quies' well built body. As the beads of water rolled off his chest and abs. Quies extended his hand to help her get up.

But as soon as she was getting up his towel dropped and she tried to cover her eyes but she was still peeking. Queis ran in the room to get dressed and Punkin had forgotten all about her phone and went back into the kitchen. She set the table and made the plates. Quies came out of the room and didn't waste any time sitting down. Thirty minutes late they were done eating and Quies told Punkin he would do the dishes while she took a shower.

She looked at him with a puzzled look and just walked off. While he was cleaning up he was also thinking of a plan to just chill with Punkin. He hurried and washed the dishes and then went to set the mood in the living room. He went through her DVDs to find a good movie for them to watch. He came across the movie "Baby Boy" he thought that would be perfect for them to watch.

Because it had everything from love to drama to comedy. That basically summed up what they were going through. Setting the TV up for the movie, he ran to his room to get his blanket off the bed.

As he was coming out of his room, Punkin was coming out at the same time. "Quies what are you doing with that blanket?"

"Well I was hoping we could watch a movie together." "Nigga, you trying to make a move on me!"

"No, I just wanted to chill with you because the only thing we do is work and come home." "Ok, but why did you get that blanket?"

"Punkin, you just got out of the shower."

"Ok, I'll go for that, but what movie are we going to be watching?" "We gonna watch Baby Boy if that's cool?"

They then sat on the sofa and Quies covered them up and hit play. Punkin kept looking at Quies the whole time, so he pulled her closer to him. When Quies pulled her closer, Punkin snuggled up under his arm and put her head on his chest. He laid his arm around her body and then looked down at her as she was already looking up at him. Punkin smiled and went back to watching the movie.

Before they knew it, they were both fast asleep on the couch in each other's arms

CHAPTER 4

The next morning when they woke up, Punkin was the first to get dressed. Quies got up with a smile on his face. He knew Punkin must have felt his morning hard on. He went and got dressed and heard someone banging on the door again. This time he beat Punkin to the door and opened it.

It wasn't who he thought it was, it was the police. When he saw them the first thing that came to his mind was run, but he knew he hadn't done anything and wasn't on probation. So he stayed to see what they wanted. As he was closing the door, Punkin came around the corner to see what was up. Quies just told her that he would fill her in on the way to work.

They both finished getting ready and headed out the door. Quies began telling her what the police wanted as they got in the car. On the way to work, Quies told Punkin how he felt about her and how he wanted to help her with her little problem with the ex. Punkin didn't want him to get involved with her ex. Arriving at the shop, Punkin and Quies saw all of the employees parked in the front.

They both were puzzled and were ready to find out what was going on. Punkin parked the car and they jumped out and ran up to the door. Walking inside, everyone started congratulating Quies. He didn't know what was going on until Shun, walked up to him and told him that he was the most requested maintenance man. Everyone that he had done a job for has called back and talked highly about him and referred him to other people.

This wasn't even on Quies' mind, all he could think about was getting his hand on a strap. He looked through the crowd to see if there was anyone he could holla at that could hook him up. But everyone there looked like they been working all their lives, until he spotted two guys standing off to the side like they could care less about what was going on. And not only that but they also looked like they were thugs trying to change like him. Quies walked over, "Excuse me y'all."

"Yeah what up?"

"Aye, I know this might sound crazy, but do one of ya'll know anybody I can get a gun from." They both looked at each other and smiled, then asked Quies if he was an undercover cop.

Quies' look said it all. So they told him to follow them outside to the van. Approaching the van one of the guys asked what kind of gun he needed, something big or small.

"Yo, if you got any type of revolver let me get it", Quies stated.

"Oh yea, I got what you need. I have a .38 special, 44 bulldog, a 357, and just a regular .38" "Shit brah, just give me the 44."

"That's what's up and thanks for shopping with us. Oh yea, and by the way my name is T-Mac and this is V.I. If you need anything else just get at one of us."

"Aight that's what's up my G." "Nawl homie we Crippin."

"Oh shit my bad cuz, but I'm good, thanks for the help."

"Oh yeah homie one more thing, we got another homie that's GD and his name is Rufus, so if you can't find us you can go to him."

"Ok that's what's up."

Quies walked to the van to put his pistol up. Then he went back inside. This time Quies spotted TMac pointing him out to some dude, he automatically knew that had to be Rufus. Quies continued as if he did not even see them. He went and picked up his paperwork so he could get started for the day.

But on the way out Punkin and Shun blocked him off. "What seems to be the rush?"

"Well if I don't work I don't get paid, and I need the money." "We really like your determination, keep up the good work." "I will do my best", Quies said as he pushed open the door. "Hey Quies, wait, wait a moment!"

"Anything for you Punkin what's up?" "Umm ... Can you umm ..."

"Can I what girl, spit it out."

"Can you come back early today?" "Yea if you need me too."

"Yeah I do, come back around 2 or 3." "Ok I got you."

Getting into the van, Quies looks over his paperwork to see if he had any specials today. It looked like he had to put in some real work today. Punching in the first job address, Quies thought he had been there before. Because he knew all about College Park. That's where he was staying before he got locked up and he hasn't been out there since he got out, so he was excited to drive through there.

Hitting the highway and heading back to the Southside brought back so many memories. He turned up the volume on the radio to hear 2 Chainz playing, that just crunked him up even more. Arriving at his destination, he parked the van and walked to the front door. Quies noticed a sign on the door that said N.O.A.M. Records. Quies walked inside to see a nigga with some long dreads talking to a high yellow chick.

"Excuse me, who do I need to talk to about the plumbing problem?" "Oh that would be me."

"Oh ok, well my name is Quies and I will be assisting you today."

"Ok Quies, I'm Trapp and the owner of N.O.A.M. Records, follow me so I can show you the problem."

"Alright, I'm right behind you. Hey Trapp, what does N.O.A.M. mean?" "It means, Niggas On A Mission."

"Oh that's hot, cause a nigga gotta stay on the grind." "Yea you feel me, but there you go right there."

Quies checked out the problem, then went and got his pipe cutter, an extra pipe, and some pipe glue. It didn't take him any time to fix the busted pipe. Once he was finished, he went to find Trapp and let him know that he was done. Trapp gave him two mix tapes for doing the job so quickly. As he was leaving the studio, he saw the high yellow chick checking him out.

But Quies just kept it moving. Hopping to the van, Quies looked at the mixtapes and put in the one called "The Green Show" by T.O. Green. He then headed to his next job. As he drove he paid attention to the radio cause this T.O. was going in. Before he knew it, he was on the Eastside and coming up on his exit. As he got off the exit he made a left onto Candler Rd. then pulled up to the McDonald's.

He walked inside the McDonald's and didn't see anything but gad chicks working in there. He went up to the counter and asked for the manager. As she walked to the front, Quies couldn't do nothing but stare at her. This woman looked like a ghetto super model with long red hair, gray eyes, and thick in all the right places. She had a butter pecan skin tone and stood about 5'7.

Quies didn't know if he wanted to do the job or just flirt. Before he could make up his mind, she had done walked up on him.

"Hi how can I help you?"

"Hi, I'm Quies from Paradise Maintenance Service." "Oh, ok I'm glad you made it, this drain is stopped up." "Ok, I can fix that in no time for you."

"Would you like something to eat when you get done?" "Yea, that would be cool."

Quies went to the van and pulled it into the back. Grabbing the tools out of the back, he headed to the side door. The manager was holding the door for him, and the way the sun was hitting her skin made her look even more amazing then she already did. The sun was making her pretty skin shin like she was an angel. Quies came back in the door and off the top he started flirting with her.

The whole time he was fixing the drain she didn't go anywhere, she just stayed there with him. Quies made her forget that she was still at work, he took her all around the world in just a short time. She didn't care if he was lying or not, cause he was feeling him just as much as he was feeling her. Everything came to an end when her boyfriend came strolling through the door. He was a big black ugly nigga, but you can tell that he had some money.

Quies kept working, but he couldn't help form looking up at this woman. As soon as he finished, she walked back to see how he was coming along. He told her he was done and was about to leave. She turned around and left, but came back with a few burgers and some fries. "Thank you for the food."

"No, thank you and anytime that you're in the area feel free to stop by." "Ok I will, and what is your name again?"

"It's Angel."

"Damn, that's the perfect name for you."

Angel could not do nothing but smile because she didn't know where her boyfriend was. She let Quies out the back door and watched him walk back to his van. He set everything at the back of the van, then went and started it up. Sitting his phone and food in the seat, he noticed that same blue Monte Carlo sitting in the parking lot. He grabbed his 44 from under his seat and put it on his hip.

Then he walked to the back of the van to put everything back in it. Closing the doors to the van, he saw Angel's boyfriend getting inside of the Monte Carlo. Quies first mind told him to pull up on dude, but he really didn't have any beef with him. Because he didn't know exactly what he was after Punkin about. Quies decided that it wasn't worth the hassle so he just jumped into the van and hauled ass.

He reached over to get his McDonalds bag and as soon as he opened it the first thing he saw was Angel's number. Quies knew that he could never have a relationship with her, because she has a man and was still giving her number out. Quies just put the number into his phone and then started to eat. Making his way down the expressway, he texted Punkin to let her know he was on the way. As he was driving he started thinking if that's the same guy and why are all these females trying to get their distance from him.

Quies was thinking to himself, "I know that nigga is ugly ass hell, but there has to be more to it". Quies felt like he was putting his captain save a hoe cape on, but he knew his situation was different with Punkin cause that's where he laid his head. So he knew he had to make her talk, he wasn't going to take no for an answer this time. Arriving back at the shop, Punkin and Shun were standing outside talking so Quies went around back and parked the van.

Quies walked up front, but before he walked out to them he stopped to see if he could hear and listen to them. The only thing he heard was them talking about how cute he was and that Punkin felt like she was falling for him, that was all he needed to hear. He then walked out the door and both of them asked, "How long have you been there?"

Quies lied and said, "Oh, I just walked up." "Well are you ready to go?"

"Yeah I guess, but where are we going?" "You will see, but we got to go to the house first." "Aight let's go cause I need to talk to you."

Punkin looked at Quies and just dropped her head. As they walked to the car, Quies looked at Punkin and saw how sexy she was looking today, but he knew he couldn't let her sexiness distract him from seeing what's up with her and her ex. Once they drove off, Quies hit her with the third degree. Punkin didn't have any other choice but to explain herself and her relationship with her ex. Quies knew it was deep but he didn't know it was that deep.

Tears started rolling down Punkin's face, Quies reached over and wiped her tears off her face. Then he told her that he was sorry about bringing it back up, but he needed to know why he is still after her. Once they got to the house, Punkin told Quies to go freshen up. He didn't ask any questions, he just did as she told him to. The whole time he was in the shower, he was thinking about the pain and trouble he caused her.

And for her to have been through all that drama and still holding herself together. From watching him kill her father and then pimping her mother, that was enough right there. Unfortunately, he did not stop there; he used to beat her, then got her pregnant and tried to set her on fire. Fucking her best friend doesn't have anything on everything else he had done to her. Just thinking about all of that mess has gotten Quies hot.

He knew he couldn't make a move on him until he tried something with him. Quies got out of the shower and put on the new outfit that Punkin had bought him. With a few sprays of cologne, Quies felt and smelled like money. As he walked out of the room, he put his 44 on his hip. Punkin was surprised on how good Quies looked when he cleaned up. "Are you ready Punkin?"

"Yes I'm ready and you're looking good for a chance." "Well thanks, you picked it out."

As they were leaving the house, Quies seen that damn Monte Carlo again. He was following them once again. Quies couldn't figure out why he kept wanting to hurt her. He didn't tell Punkin that he was behind them because he didn't want to freak her out. He just made sure he kept an eye on the car while they were driving into downtown traffic.

Because he thought she might have a chance to lose them, but Quies wasn't sure on where they were heading too. Next thing he knew, Punkin was getting off the Atlantic Station exit. She found a parking spot in no time. Quies continued to look around to see if he saw the Monte Carlo, but it was nowhere in sight. As they got out of the car, Quies walked over and put his arm around Punkin.

He knew that they weren't together, but she was looking too good for him not to put on like she was his. She just looked at him and smiled. Punkin never really had someone do the things to her like Quies does, and that made her feel very comfortable. Walking into Fox Sports and Grill, Punkin told the waiter that she needed a table for two. The waiter told them to follow him; he sat them at a table by the window.

Glancing at the menu, Quies was ready to order. Punkin also knew what she wanted. The waiter returned and they both placed their order. While waiting for their food, Quies began hitting on Punkin, but she was used to niggas running game. Punkin felt like he just wanted to try and get some when they returned home. As they spent a few hours eating and talking they had a visitor come to the table.

"Hi Quies."

"Hey Sanaa, how are you?" "I'm doing good and you?"

"Well that's good to know. Umm ... Punkin this is Sanaa, Sanaa this is Punkin." "How are you?"

Quies seen the look on Punkin's face, he knew he had to send Sanaa on about her business. As Sanaa walked away from the table, he tried his hardest not to watch her walk away, but she was looking better than before, she was all dressed up this time around. The dress she had on was showing every curve, which made it tough for any man not to look. Quies took a quick peek, and then told Punkin that Sanaa was just a customer, but not a special customer. That made her feel a little bit better, but she was still ready to go after that.

Leaving out of the restaurant, Punkin took and gripped Quies' hand while walking out the door. She knew she had to let it be known that she was feeling him, cause after she saw Sanaa she felt like she might lose him. Punkin knew she was a bad chick, but Sanaa made her feel a little unsure. As they walked around Atlantic Station, they begun to feel and look like a real couple. Quies started getting all type of weird signs, and before he could tell Punkin, he was ready to go; her ex-boyfriend was coming down the sidewalk.

Punkin froze up and grabbed Quies by the arm extra tight. "Come here you little bitch!" Her ex-boyfriend yelled."

"Hold on homie, what's your problem? You need to watch your mouth." Quies said to him. Her ex responded, "Look here you little pussy, this ain't got nothing to do with you, so fall back!" "Well I hate to tell you this, but you just put me in it. So whatever ya'll had going on before me, that's over with now."

"You bitch ass nigga, didn't I just tell you to stay in your place!"

Before Quies knew it, he had hit that nigga in the mouth. They began fighting up and down the sidewalk. All Punkin could do was scream for them to stop, but Quies had blacked out and kicked into combat mode. Quies tried not to get hit because her ex-boyfriend was a big dude.

When Quies had the chance he told Punkin to hurry up and get to the car. He knew it wouldn't be much longer before the cops showed up.

Punkin ran to get the car while they were still going at it. The ex-boyfriend rushed in and grabbed Quies and took him to the ground. As they fell to the ground, Quies's pistol fell of his hip and went off. The Ex-friend thought he was shot, so him and Quies jumped to their feet asap. Quies picked up the 44 and aimed it at him and everyone starting screaming and freaking out, taking off running in all directions.

Punkin showed up just in time, Quies hopped inside the car and Punkin hit the gas. Punkin called Shun to see if it was cool for them to come over and stay the night. Punkin didn't want to go home, because she didn't want things to get out of hand. She knew her ex would show up after all that happened. All she kept thinking about was to save Quies because he stood up for her.

Approaching Shun's house, Punkin called Shun to let her know that they were pulling up in about five minutes. Then she looked at Quies and told him thanks for standing up for her. Quies just gave her a look like she was going to pay for it, but he couldn't stay mad at her so he just smiled and told her she's welcome.

CHAPTER 5

"Hey y'all!"

"What's up Shun." Quies and Punking replied. Entering in the house, Shun knew something was wrong. She made them as comfortable as possible. Shun stayed in a big house by herself, and she loved it when she had company. Quies' mind was on getting cleaned up, so he didn't want to talk. He asked Shun if she had some sweat pants that he could put on so he could take a shower.

Shun looked at him like he was crazy. Punkin told her that he has been fighting.

Shun's attitude changed and told him to wait a minute so she could find him some. Punkin got off the sofa and went and sat with Quies on the love seat. Reaching for his hand she couldn't stop thinking about what had happened, but what she realized was that she was dealing with a real man.

Since day one, Quies has been trying to help her. She looked at Quies and grabbed his face with her other hand and told him thank you again, she then gave him a kiss on his lips. Shun walked in and cleared her throat and said, "Am I interrupting anything?" Punkin jumped like she was 16 and just got caught kissing a boy, by her mother and father. Shun started laughing at her as she threw Quies an old pair of sweats, a tower, and a wash rag. Quies asked where the bathroom was, and while heading to the bathroom he was checking her house out.

He thought to himself, "Damn, she is making good money with the shop." The bathroom was extremely bright, everything was white and silver. Quies then set his stuff on the counter and got into the shower.

Meanwhile, Punkin and Shun were sitting in the living room talking about what happened tonight. Punkin told every detail as they drank some wine.

The more Punkin told Shun about Quies, the more she started to realize how much she liked Quies. She was trying to find out if they had slept together yet or not, but she didn't want to come straight out and ask her because they had a rule of not sleeping with any of the employees. There was something about Quies that made her want to break the rule. Punkin didn't tell Shun that she was falling in-love with Quies. Punkin didn't want to break the rules either, but she didn't know that Shun wanted to break them too.

Quies walked into the living room with his shirt off and everything got quiet. Punkin and Shun looked at each other and then back at Quies. Punkin wanted to tell him to put his shirt on but she didn't want Shun to think that it was more then what she had told her. Quies knew that they had been talking about him cause every time they get together and he is around, that's what they do. He asked Shun if she had a shirt he could put on and if she could wash his outfit.

Shun smiled, and told him that he was going to pay for her working like this. As he handed her his clothes, Shun winked at him and walked off. He went and sat next to Punkin to make sure she was ok. Shun walked in and gave him a T-Shirt that she slept in. He put the shirt on and started yawning. He was exhausted from working and then having that fight with Punkin's ex.

He sat back down to talk to them for a few minutes, and before he knew it he was out like a light. Punkin go up so he could stretch all the way out. Then, her and Shun went to the bedroom and continued talking about work and everything that's been going on. Punkin began to get tired herself, so she got some things from Shun and went and took a shower. Shun went to take Quies a blanket and to put his things in the dryer.

As she covered him, thoughts of them having sex went through her mind. She was imagining wrapping her lips around his cock and sucking it until he was rock hard. Then she would get on top of him and ride him like a roller coaster. Now she felt herself getting wet just thinking about it. Shun was almost ready to just put it on him, but she heard the water from the shower shut off.

Shun ran back to the room before Punkin came out of the bathroom. She turned on the T.V. and got in the bed. Punkin came out and jumped right into bed with Shun. She laid there for a few minutes and then she started thinking about Quies, she jumped out of the bed and ran to check on him. He was still sound asleep so she kissed him one last time.

Walking back into the bedroom, Shun had cut everything off. Punkin was unable to do anything as she walked to the bed. Once she got into the bed, Punkin felt Shun reaching for her under the covers. Punkin was thinking that it has been a long time since the last time they messed around. Punkin thought they would never mess around again because both of them agreed to put that behind them.

But Shun wasn't letting up. Shun crawled over to Punkin and slid her panties to the side. Shun began licking and playing with her clit. Punkin grabbed the top of her head pulling her hair as she got in her zone. Shun stuck one of her fingers in at a upward motion, like she was telling someone to come here. Hitting her G-spot, Punkin couldn't do anything but pull harder on Shun's hair.

Shun took off her panties and put her pussy in Punkin's face. While in the 69, Punkin returned the favor. Punkin reached over to Shun's nightstand and pulled out one of the dildo's and began sliding it in and out of Shun.Within a few minutes Shun climaxed. Shun was so wet, she was dripping cum all over Punkin's tits.

Shun was moaning louder and louder. Punkin realized the door was open, so she stopped because she didn't want to wake Quies. Punkin made Shun get up and close the door, but Shun didn't want to because she wanted Quies to wake up and join. As she got back into bed, Punkin began sucking on her breasts and kissing all over her. Shun laid back and Punkin strapped on the dildo, she then slid it inside her.

Punkin began pounding her pussy until she squirted everywhere. Punkin immediately pulled out the dildo and went straight to sucking on her clit and playing with her nipples. Shun pushed Punkin off her and strapped up with the dildo. She still had cum dripping down her leg, but she didn't even care. She flipped Punkin over and started hitting it from the back.

Shun was always crazy about Punkin's ass. She gripped and smacked her ass while she banged her from behind. Then she took her thumb and worked it inside of Punkin's ass. Punkin got wetter and wetter and started throwing her ass back harder and harder. Shun took her other hand and grabbed Punkin's hair and started pulling on it.

Punkin couldn't take too much, she began scooting up the bed. Shun flipped her over and put her in the buck just like Punkin did her. Shun was sexing her like she was a dude. Punkin forgot all about

Quies, she started screaming as she reached her climax. Shun went even harder and faster until Punkin started pushing her off of her.

Shun pulled out and took off the dildo, and went to get a warm rag to clean up.

Punkin laid in the bed while Shun cleaned her up. Once she got done, she put the rag on the night stand and got in the bed next to Punkin. They started laughing at each other about what just went down. They laughed and talked about how they were fucking until they fell asleep.

CHAPTER 6

The next morning when Quies woke up he looked around to see if Shun and Punkin was asleep on the sofa. The only thing he saw was his clothes. He got dressed and then went to the bathroom to freshen up. When he came out he went back to the living room to sit down. As he was getting comfortable, Shun and Punkin came walking out of the bedroom in their panties and bra.

He didn't say a thing, he just sat there as they walked to the kitchen. Quies then crept up on them watching them laugh and giggle about last night. Not knowing he was behind them, Shun bent over to get something out of the refrigerator. Quies saw her fat pussy poking out in her panties and before he could stop himself he said "Damn" out loud. Shun and Punkin both jumped and turned around to see Quies standing there holding himself.

Shun gave him a little show and made her ass clap, while Punkin turned and acted shy. Then she pulled Shun towards her and dragged her off to the room so they could get dressed for work. Quies watched them both as they walked down the hallway. He thought it would be fun to have sex with both of them because they were both fine as hell. He did know that Punkin wouldn't go for it, but wasn't sure how Shun would be.

Quies still hasn't figured why Punkin hasn't made her move yet on him because he knew she was feeling him. Hell, Shun was way more open then Punkin was. Since the beginning, Quies has been trying to be a gentleman because she's been there for him when he needed her. He stopped thinking about it because he knew it wouldn't ever happen. Punkin and Shun came back up front ready to go.

As they left the house, Quies watched to see if anyone was following them. Punkin looked at Quies and asked him if he liked Shun. He didn't know if he should answer that or not. He played it cool and kept it real, he told her he thought that Shun was sexy and all, but she wasn't Punkin. Punkin liked that answer so she didn't ask him anything else.

She just turned the radio up cause she loved listening to the Rickey Smiley Morning Show. It was quite ironic too because they were talking about relationships. Punkin glanced over at Quies to see if he was paying attention, but he was ready to get to work so he could take his mind off all the bullshit that happened last night. Driving up to the shop, Quies saw everybody waiting for them to get there. Shun had pulled up two minutes before they did.

As they parked the car, Quies looked at Punkin and asked her if she was going to make her move. But she didn't know what he was talking about. Quies got out of the car and left her to ponder on what he just asked her. He went inside to get his paperwork for the day, then went out back to get his van. About time Punkin made it inside, Quies was already gone. She wanted to tell him the answer to this question, but it was too late.

Shun walked and showed Punkin all of the work orders that they had. They were falling behind and they needed to work late today. Quies noticed that he didn't have any specials today, so he thought the jobs he had must be really hard. He didn't care, as long as he got to make some money and be around beautiful women. It didn't take him long to get to his first job.

Once he got inside the house it didn't take him no time to fix the problem. He went through his jobs quicker than he thought he would. The faster he was knocking out the jobs, the faster

Shun or Punkin would call him with more. The day had flown by and Quies had one more job to do before he could go home. He grabbed his last Red bull and took it to the head.

Then typed in the address on the GPS, because he ain't ever heard of this spot and he's been all over ATLANTA. Focusing back on the road, he thought he was being followed. But this time it wasn't the blue Monte Carlos so he thought he was just tripping because he was tired. The only thing kept him going was the thought of him letting Punkin down. He was a man of his word and he knew he couldn't let her down.

That gave him more motivation to go and get the job done. Quies hit the gas so he could cover some more ground. Before he realized he had been driving for an hour and a half, and he was just coming up on his exit. As he got off the highway his phone rang.

"Hello."

"Quies where are you?"

"I'm on my way to the last job, what's up?" "Oh nothing just wanted to check on you." "Oh, so what are you really trying to say, you miss me?"

"Boy, whatever, it ain't like that."

"Oh so you're saying you don't miss me." "Quies you know I miss you a little bit." "Ok, that's all I wanted to hear."

"Well I'm at the house, just call me when you are on the way."

"Ok I will, but I have to go because I am pulling up at the customer's house now." "Ok."

The same car that was following Quies on the highway parked two houses down. Queis thought it was funny because he knew that the car was following him. He rang the doorbell; it took the customer about five minutes to come to the door. As the door opened, there were two chicks standing in the doorway. One was dark chocolate and the other Asian.

They grabbed Quies by his hands and pulled him in the house and shut the door. He didn't even have to say who he was. They took him into the room that had all types of toys. Quies just knew he was in for a treat, he asked for their names. The chocolate chick's name was Miracle and the Asian's name was Juicy.

Quies thought they had their names mixed up, because the Asian wasn't juicy at all, but he didn't say anything. They sat him in a chair that they had in the room. Then Miracle hit the play button on the radio. They both began dancing and stripping for him. They pulled Quies out of his seat and stripped him naked while they were still dancing for him.

They then proceeded to sit him back in the chair. Miracle started making her ass clap while Juicy was under her on her knees doing the same thing. Miracle walked backwards while her ass was still giggling. She sat on Quies' lap and grinded up and down on him. As Quies' cock started to swell, Miracle placed it inside of her.

She grinded on him and Juicy came crawling on her knees and started licking her clit and sucking on his balls. Quies got harder then Superman's knee cap. Miracle stood up leaving her juices all on his swollen cock. Juicy came and went straight down on it, kissing his head then deep throating him. Juicy looked up at him while she was bobbing up and down.

Miracle had gone and got on the bed and began playing with herself. Juicy got up and took Quies by his hand and led him to the bed. As she climbed on the bed, she kissed and licked Miracle up her legs until she was able to slip her tongue inside of her wet kitty. While she was doing that, Quies slapped her ass as he placed himself inside of her. Juicy jumped a little bit because he was more then she was used to.

As Quies worked his magic, he saw where Juicy got her name from. He gripped her by her hips and brought her closer to him with each stroke. Juicy shot out large amounts of cum the harder Quies got. He pulled out and pulled Miracle to him. Her ass was hanging off the edge of the bed and Quies went right up in her.

Using his other hand, he picked up the toy she was using before he came to the bed and started playing with Juicy with it. He had both of them gripping the sheets. The harder and faster he went on Miracle, the crazier her faces got and the more she sucked on her breasts. Quies flipped her over and laid her on her back and picked up Juicy and sat her on top of her. He would then hit juicy from the back and pull out and go straight into Miracle.

He went back and forth with them for a few minutes. Then he switched them around. Juicy couldn't take it, she squirmed and wiggled until he couldn't put it in her anymore. Then Juicy and Miracle both got up and gave Quies some service. They took turns trying to see who could do it better, trying to get him to cum in their mouths.

They couldn't get him too, so they put him on the bed. Miracle got on top of him and bounced up and down, side to side in a circular motion while squeezing her kitty muscle. Juicy was riding his face while he was playing with her breast. They had him stretched out in every way you could think of. Miracle began to bounce faster and faster as she reached her climax, her moans turned into soft sensual screams of "I'm cumming!".

She got up to let Juicy have her turn, and she took Juicy's spot. Juicy got up there and started riding Quies. She turned around so Quies could see her ass go up and down.

As she goes up, she tightens her kitty muscle, squeezing Quies' rock hard cock. When she gets to his head she squeezes even tighter.

When she feels like she is about to come out, she loosens up and goes back down. Quies is feeling so good his toes are beginning to curl. Juicy speeds up reaching her climax, and when she does she stands up and squirts cum all over Quies. Quies gets up and grabs Juicy; he puts her in the buck position and drills her as hard as he could. Knowing that she couldn't take it, he wouldn't let her up.

Quies got faster and faster until he reached his peak. He pulled out and ejaculated all over their faces. They were catching cum like two dogs,were drinking at a water fountain. Quies finished up and asked for a wash rag to clean up. Juicy went to get a warm rag with soap so everyone could clean up, but Miracle wasn't done.

She bent over to Quies and started sucking him again. Quies raised up on his tiptoes because he was tender. Miracle started working on just the head, and before they knew it Quies started cumming again. Juicy already was cleaned up so she gave them a hand and wiped Miracle first then Quies. As she cleaned him up she was kissing every inch of his body.

Quies felt himself getting hard again, he knew he had to get out of there though. He soon got dressed and walked to the door with both of them tailing him. As he walked out the door Miracle and Juicy told him to make sure he came back. "So that means y'all had fun?" Quies asked. The both smiled and said they wanted more.

Quies wouldn't have minded going another round, but he was beat and it was really late, going on nine o'clock. He had been there since 6:30 pm. Quies told them that he would love to but he really had to make it back to Atlanta. They looked at him with the sad puppy dog face and told him goodnight. Quies got in the van and didn't waste any time pulling off.

The closer he got to the expressway the more he realized he had to get some gas. While getting gas, he went to the chicken restaurant inside and ordered some chicken to go. He started eating while waiting for the van to fill up. Quies got back into the van and reached over to get his phone out of the glove department just to see if he had any missed calls. He saw that he had 15 missed calls, all from Punkin.

She had left him 3 voicemails. As he checked them, the gas pump stopped. He stepped out and put the gas nozzle up, got back in the van and drove off. As he started his messages over he heard how the messages had changed. Quies hit the gas trying to make it back up the highway.

He was getting fed up with Punkin's ex. Feeling up under his seat, Quies grabbed his 44 and put it in his lap. The only thing he could think about was knocking him off and putting an end to this bullshit. All kinds of crazy ways to kill him kept popping into his head. Before he realized it he was back in the city, but didn't take his foot off the gas.

He took that hour and half and turned it into 45 minutes. Quies was determined to get to Punkin before anything could happen to her. As he drove down his street he made sure he didn't see anybody outside or even that Monte Carlo. Everything was a little too quiet for Quies. He jumped out the van with the pistol in his hand.

As he went to the front door, he was checking to see if there was anything wrong with it. But there was no sign of a break-in. Before he could knock, shots were fired. He jumped in the bushes hoping that he wouldn't get hit. As he crawled through the bushes trying to make his way back to the van, he wanted to see where the shots came from.

Once he came out of the bushes, shots rang out again. This time he was able to see where they were coming from, so returned fire. Quies had to get out of there ASAP because he didn't have much ammunition. Now he was wishing that he had another pistol. He got into the van and turned it the key and hit the gas, ducking down so he wouldn't get hit.

Even though the faster he drove, it seemed like more shots were coming, like he'd been ambushed. Quies got to the end of the street and didn't slow down, he hit a hard right and it felt like he was on two wheels.

Once he made it off the street, he looked for his phone. The phone was sliding around on the floor, so he picked it up. He called Punkin. Her phone kept ringing, but then she finally picked up.

"Yo Punkin where the fuck you at?"

"I'm at Shun's house, I couldn't stay at my house."

"Yea, I can see that. That fuck nigga just shot up my van." "Oh my God Quies, are you ok?"

"Yea, I'm good, but how did you get out of the house?"

"I watched them leave and I jumped in the car and hauled ass. I didn't know if they were coming back or not."

"Ok, well you stay there I'll call you later." "Quies, where you going?" "I can't tell you, but I'll call you later."

"Baby, please be safe." Quies called T-Mac.

"Yo!"

"What's up brah, this Quies." "Oh, what's crackin cuz?"

"Aye man I need some heat, the 44 doesn't have enough rounds." "Aight, I got you tomorrow."

"Nawl my nigga, I need something tonight, these niggas just tried to take me out." "Ok say no more, meet me at the shop in 5." "I'll be there in 2."

As they hung up the phone, Quies was thinking how he was going to make it back over there without them seeing him. He pulled up at the shop and T-Mac was already there in a cripped out Box Chevy sitting on 26's. He told Quies to park the van and hop in. As he got into the car,

T-Mac pulled off. "What's crackin cuz?"

"Man, I just got in to a shootout; well really I just got ambushed by some niggas." "Dam cuz, so what type of heat you looking for?"

"I need something small that has a lot of rounds." "Aight I got just the thing for you."

T-Mac gave Quies a F-N with an extra clip. Then he dropped him back off at the shop. Quies got into the van and went to the house. Quies didn't pull up on the street, he parked the van on down the road and went through the woods. Creeping up on the house, Quies was waiting to see someone out of place.

Quies kept a watch on the house and the road, but next thing you know Quies was fast asleep.

CHAPTER 7

The next morning Quies woke up by the vibration of his phone. He jumped and went to reaching for both of his pistols. As he looked around he had forgotten that he had fallen asleep outside. He went in his pocket to get his phone to see who was calling him. It was Punkin trying to see where he was at because she was standing beside his van.

Quies told her that he was at the house and he needed to get in. Punkin flew to the house. Quies was standing by the mailbox as Punkin pulled in the driveway. He walked up to the house and they went inside. He went to his room to get some clothes and to put his guns up.

As he got in the shower, Punkin came knocking on the door. He stuck his arm out of the shower to unlock the door. Punkin came in and sat on the toilet and began asking him what happened last night and why the van is parked in the parking lot. He told her everything from how he wanted to make sure nothing happened to her, to the part where he got ambushed. He just didn't tell her about where he got his guns from, because he didn't want to bring no heat on T-Mac and the crew.

Punkin sat on the toilet and began crying. She hasn't ever felt so loved before. But she just didn't know she was on the verge of losing Quies. He was willing to help her out cause she helped him. But shit had done got crazy for him and he ain't even hit it yet.

He knew she liked him and wanted to be with him, but he didn't want to make the first move. She told him when he first moved in that she was just helping him because of his situation. So he never tried to cross that line with her. He turned off the shower and stepped out with his towel wrapped around him. Punkin stood and put her head on his chest.

Quies grabbed her and told her everything is going to be ok. Punkin looked up at Quies then started kissing on him. Quies gripped Punkin by her ass and set her on the bathroom counter. Kissing on her and gripping her ass made her get hot. Punkin started undressing while she was still kissing.

Quies got rock hard and tried to work his way inside of her. But she was sitting too far back, Quies pulled her closer to him and went right in. Taking a few strokes inside Punkin, she got wet like rain water. She grasped him around the neck and started grinding the best she could from on top of the counter. Then she thought about having to go to work, she pushed Quies off of her and jumped off the counter.

Punkin tried to leave out the bathroom but Quies grabbed her and bent her over in the middle of the hallway. And went back to work, Punkin leaned over more and wrapped her hands around her ankles. Then started throwing it back, it was feeling so good she didn't want to stop. She knew she couldn't be late for work, so she felt Quies pulling back. She broke loose and ran to her room.

Before Quies had got to the door she had shut and locked it. "Quies we got to go to work. We can't do this right now."

"So you're going to do me like that Punkin?" "Quies I'm sorry but we got to go to work. I'll make it up to you somehow."

"Man you know that's fucked up right, I am not going to forget about this", Quies said as he walked off.

Quies went to his room mad as hell. He quickly got dressed and went to the living room to wait for Punkin. Punkin came out of her room shortly after he did and they left. Punkin took Quies to pick up the van. He jumped out of the car and didn't say anything to her; he just got in the van and drove off.

Arriving at the shop, Quies went in to get his paperwork. Shun asked him if he had seen Punkin? He looked at her with a fuck you look and told her that she was on the way. Shun didn't know what had happened with Quies but she could tell he was pissed. Quies got his paperwork and hit the door.

As he was walking to the Van Punkin was just pulling up. He didn't even look her way, he got in the van and drove off. Quies typed the address into the GPS and he knew that address but he couldn't remember who lived there. While Quies was driving he leaned up and took the F-N off his hip and put it under his seat. He didn't want to forget about it and walk into the customer's house.

But he didn't want to get caught without it either. Thirty minutes later he was pulling up at his job site and he knew where he was. His whole mood had done changed. Quies walked up to the door and Kimberly was standing there waiting on him. They walked in the house and Kimberly took Quies into the living room.

That threw him for a loop; he was expecting to go to the room. Kim pushed him down on the sofa and dropped her robe. She was standing in a green and white teddy with her hair down. She slowly strutted closer to the sofa and put one of her legs on the edge of the couch. Draped over Quies with her hair in his face.

Then engaged in kissing all over him, taking off his clothes while she worked her kisses down his body. Then placed Quies erect penis inside of her. Slowly going up and down on him. She wrapped her arms around his neck as she speeded up. Quies wiggled his way to the edge of the sofa and stood up with Kim still on him.

Bouncing her up and down then laid her on the couch and began grinding on her. Kim softly moaned to Quies for him to go harder. Quies had forgotten that Kim was a pain freak. So he started jabbing her pussy like he was playing Mike Tyson punch out. Kim wrapped her legs around him and tried to throw it back.

Quies flipped her over as he stood up and placed her on the arm of the couch. Then grabbed her by the back of her neck and pulled her back with force as he trusted himself inside her. Quies went from grabbing her neck and pulling her hair and smacking her ass. Quies was thrashing Kim on the couch. He was screwing her so good she yelled out I love you.

But Quies didn't pay her any attention, he just started going harder. Kim was cumming so much it was running down both her legs. As Quies felt himself about to climax, he pulled out and went straight in Kim's ass. Releasing all in her, Kim told him that she loved him once again. Quies removed himself out of her ass and put it right in her mouth.

Kim sucked him until he came in her mouth and on her face. Kim got up to go clean her face off, Quies quickly got dressed cause he knew Kim wasn't going to let him go that easy. Once he got dressed he made his way out the door before Kim came back. He got in the van and drove off, but he didn't know Kim was on his tail. She had got on a moped to follow him.

Just so happens Quies looked in his rearview mirror and saw her. He sped up and left her in the middle of the street looking crazy once again. Quies just started laughing to himself because he couldn't believe she chased him again. Kim was a good fuck, but she was just too crazy for him. Quies got his paperwork to see where his next job was located at.

He rode down the highway, and Sanna popped in his head. Quies took out his phone and called her up, but she didn't answer. Quies called her back again hoping she would pick up this time, but just to his luck she didn't pick up again, so he left her a message. "Yo Sanaa, this is yo boy Quies, I'm trying to get up with you so hit me up." Quies laid his phone in his lap hoping that she would call him right back.

As Quies was getting off the expressway, he saw that Monte Carlo sitting at the light with nobody around. Quies reached under his seat to grab his gun. He just wanted to send some shots that nigga's way. It made it even better for him because he was going in the opposite direction. Quies let down the window and as he drove by he let the 44 rip, they both hit the gas ASAP.

At this point, Quies didn't even care if he even killed him right then. It would have just been one less problem that he had to worry about. Quies put the 44 in the glove box and kept the F-N under the seat. Approaching the next job Quies made sure that he wasn't being followed. He parked the van behind some bushes just in case old boy drove through looking for him.

Walking inside the office he immediately knew that he was gonna be there for awhile. The carpet was soak and wet. Quies spotted a dude walking around in the back of the office. So he walked to where the man was at to see if he was the one that called.

"Excuse me sir, I'm here from Paradise Maintenance Service and I was trying to see if you were the one that called."

"Yes I am, I'm sure you can see we really need your help."

"Ok well that's why I'm here, just show me that problem and I'll fix it." "Ok right this way, and my name is Henry in case you need anything." "Aight Mr.Henry, I'm Quies."

Henry showed Quies where the problems were. It was a multiple pipe bust. Quies had to turn the water off to the whole building. Then he went and got his tools that he needed. Quies was about ten minutes into the job when he spotted a box that had four bottles of acid in them. He stopped working and grabbed a bottle and took it to the van and came back to work.

Three and half hours later Quies was just finishing up. He took all his tools back to the van and told Henry he was finished. He got into the van and drove off. He picked up his phone to see if he had any missed calls, he had one. Hoping it was Sanaa, but realized it was only the shop. He called the shop to see what was up, Shun picked up.

"Thanks for calling Paradise Maintenance Service." "Aye this is Quies I had a miss call from the shop."

"Oh yea, Quies you don't have to come in tomorrow, I'm letting you and Punkin have the day off."

"Ok that's what's up, can you let her know that I'm on the way back?" "Yea I got you."

Thirty minutes later Quies pulled up at the shop and Punkin was waiting on him like always. He parked the van and wiped it down, then grabbed both of his pistols. As soon as he got ready to walk around front, Punkin drove up to see what was taking him so long. Quies just jumped in the car, and the first thing Punkin said was she was sorry about earlier and then she pulled off. Quies looked at her and just nodded his head.

On the way home, Punkin stopped at Checker's so they could get something to eat. Punkin ordered her food and then Quies got the two for three spicy chicken sandwiches with chili cheese fries and a milkshake. Punkin looked over at him and said, "Damn nigga, you that hungry." Queis couldn't do anything but laugh. Once they got their food they went straight home.

As they walked inside the house, Quies went to his room and closed the door. He had to hide his pistols and reload one of them. Punkin came and banged on his door until he opened it. "Dam nigga, you ain't got no kicking it for a bitch, I told you I was sorry."

"Shawty you trippin, I had to handle some business, I'm about to come and kick it with yo stanking ass."

"Whatever, you know you like all of this." Quies walked behind Punkin as they walked to the living room. Now Punkin wanted to watch a movie so she could make her move on Quies. But what she didn't know is that Quies was already plotting on her. While they ate and watched their movie, Quies saw Punkin looking at him. Quies leaned and started kissing Punkin.

Quies started to take her clothes off so he could kiss her body. He was trying his hardest not to smile. Making his way down her body and started giving her oral sex. Quies saw how she was getting into it and getting all worked up. He stopped and ran to his room and locked the door.

He knew she was going to be mad. Punkin came to the door and cursed him out and kept beating on the door for him to come out, but Quies got into bed and went to sleep.

CHAPTER 8

Waking up the next day, Quies was feeling good about himself. But he knew Punkin was going to be mad because of what happened last night. So Quies decided he was going to plan a date night for the both of them. It was already 11:00 am, so he went and took a shower. The whole time he was in the shower he was thinking, how to make his plan better than it already was.

Quies made his way out of the shower and walked to his room with the tower wrapped around him. But before he could make it, Punkin stopped him. She gripped Quies on his ass and told him that he was going to give her some of that dick. Quies laughed at her and walked in the room. While walking past Punkin, Quies told her to get dressed because they were going out today.

Then he shut the door in her face.

Punkin went to her room and got dressed as Quies demanded. Meanwhile, Quies was in his room going through all of his clothes trying to see what he wanted to wear. Getting paid every week with bonuses on Friday's helped Quies get all the way right. He finally pulled out a TRUE Religion outfit with a fresh pair of Balise, then got dressed. Before coming out of his room, he sprayed on some Polo Black.

He knocked on Punkin's door, when she opened it up she looked like a supermodel. Quies asked her if she was ready to go, Punkin looked at him and told him she still needed to do her hair. He had told her not to worry about it because he would take her to get it done if that was ok with her. Punkin smiled and said ok.

They left the house and went straight to Alexis's Whacky Weave Hair Salon. When they arrived, Quies pulled right up front. He got out of the car and went inside to holla at Alexis. When he came back out he told Punkin to go inside and ask for Alexis. And told her to call him when she was done, so he could come and pick her up.

Quies drove off to finish up planning for the rest of their day together. Quies was planning a romantic evening for the both of them. He drove around the streets of Atlanta shopping for things to set the mood at the house. Once he was done shopping, he went back to the house and set everything up. When Quies finished up, the phone rang and she was done.

Quies grabbed his F-N and the keys and hit the door. He forgot it the first time, but he didn't want to this time. He didn't know what might happen when they hit the streets.

Quies didn't waste any time getting back to the hair salon. As he was approaching the parking lot, Punkin walked outside to wait on him.

Quies pulled up and gave Punkin curbside service. As he opened the car door for her, all the ladies in the salon were just watching. Quies turned around and blew a kiss at them and got back in the car smiling. Punkin was looking and smelling so good, Quies knew what was up. They took off and hit the expressway heading to downtown Atlanta.

Once they made it downtown, Quies drove around until they got to the Georgia Aquarium. Quies parked the car and they went inside. Walking around looking at all the different fish and watching all the shows, had made the both of them hungry. Quies took her to the restaurant inside the aquarium. As they ate and talked, the more Punkin realized how much she liked Quies.

Once they were finished eating they left the aquarium. Punkin thought that their date was over for the night, but Quies pulled up next to Centennial Park and parked on the side of the road. Quies took her for a walk around the park, so they could view the city at night with all its beautiful lights on display. Punkin saw all the couples walking around holding hands. She felt extra special cause Quies had his arm around her.

Quies took her to the ferris-wheel so they could enjoy the night in the sky. Sitting at the top of the ferris-wheel looking at the lights and the stars made Punkin feel like she was on top of the world. Quies leaned over and kissed her on her forehead, right after the kiss Punkin snuggled in closer to Quies and put her head on his chest.

The ferris-wheel slowly worked its way back around so they could get off. After helping Punkin off, they proceeded to walk back to the car. Out of nowhere, Punkin's ex-boyfriend showed up. Queis was hoping that he had killed that nigga that day he shot up the car.

"Yo pussy, I bet you thought I was dead, didn't you?"

"Man what the fuck you want now, what you want to fight again?"

"Nawl fuck boy, you gonna die tonight." Punkin yelled out, "Patrick no, don't kill him." "Bitch, what I did told you about getting in my business."

Quies told Punkin to stay out of it and go to the car. As soon as she walked off, Patrick's homeboys walked up.

"Yo Pat, what do you want us to do with this fool?" "Beat that nigga's ass, then I'm gonna off him."

Quies didn't waste any time he bombed on the closest nigga to him and the others jumped in to help. Quies was going in on them. He had been jumped a few times prior, so fighting three or more people wasn't nothing to him. Quies knew that they would get the best of him, but they would know that he was there. Quies was handling three of them pretty good, so Pat jumped in.

Pat blindsided Quies and sent him to his knees. While Quies was on his knees, Pat's homeboys started kicking him. The only thing Quies could do was keep on throwing punches and kicking back hoping that Punkin would show up soon with the car. The only one really doing anything to Quies was Pat, so he knew he had to take him out.

Before he knew it, Quies heard police coming and people screaming, "He's got a gun." Quies knew it was over with for him, until he heard Punkin's sexy voice telling him to run. Quies ran to the car and Pat didn't let up off the trigger. Quies luckily was able to jump into the car. Quies reached under the seat and grabbed his F-N.

He stuck it out the window and started shooting, Quies didn't care who he hit. Bullets were flying everywhere, hitting parked cars, trees, and who knows what else.

Just at the right time, Quies pulled back into the when two Atlanta Police came flying down the street. Punkin was so scared she could not stop shaking. Quies told her to calm down and call Shun, and to see if they could come over.

Quies knew God was on his side tonight, cause he didn't get hit one time while Pat was shooting. On top of that, they had hit all green lights on the way out. Quies knew if Shun wouldn't let them over there they couldn't go home. Quies asked Punkin if it was cool that they went there, and Punkin just shook her head yes. Quies figured he would check his clip and see what was left since Punkin was on the phone.

He pulled the clip out of the gun and Pun kin got scared all over again. Quies told her to calm down, he was about to put it up.

Quies was fed up with all this shit he was going through with Punkin and that nigga Pat. He was so ready to put an end to all of this shit, but he just didn't know how he was going to do it yet. Quies' mind was racing through ideas.

As they arrived at Shun's house Quies grabbed his F-N and put it on his hip. Punkin begged him to leave it in the car, but Quies wasn't going for that. He told her that he felt safer with it on him because he never knew when Pat might show up. Shun opened the door and heard them fussing about the gun. She just told them to come in with it.

Shun looked at Quies and told him that he always stays in something. Quies couldn't even say anything because it was all because of Punkin. Shun kept talking to Quies but he had done zoned out, thinking about why he kept his life on the line for her. It was fun for him at first, cause he thought the first fight was going to get Pat to leave her alone. Unfortunately, this nigga is like the Terminator, he just keeps coming back.

Quies was thinking that Punkin must had some good pussy or that nigga is crazy.Quies snapped out of this thoughts, as Shun gave him a little push cause she realized that he wasn't paying attention to her. "Oh my bad Shun I was in deep thought", Quies said. Shun turned on the TV as they sat in the living room and began to talk. Just as they started talking they caught the news.

It was breaking news on Fox 5. Somebody had recorded Quies getting his ass beat, but you really could not make his face out clearly. Quies wasn't mad about them recording him. He was just mad that they only recorded the part, when they were getting the best of him. Shun started joking with Quies about how they whipped his ass.

Quies just let her have it cause he knew he was busting those nigga's up. Before Shun could say anything else, they showed another video clip of the whole thing. When they got to the part of them showing Pat pull the gun, all you could see was the ground and some tennis shoes. The news reporter said that they had two suspects in custody, but no names yet, they were still looking for the others. Quies just dropped his head and prayed that they couldn't see his face.

Punkin leaned over and started rubbing Quies on his back and telling him that it was going to be ok. Shun got up to get him a towel and wash rag so he could clean up. She knew he needed a hot shower so he could relax. Quies left them in the living room as he went to take his shower. Fifteen minutes later, Quies was good and soapy and heard a knock on the door.

He yelled, "Come in!" and kept bathing. He thought it was Punkin coming to give him his clothes, but he was surprised. Quies felt something warm wrap around his dick and start jacking him. Quies quickly washed the soap out of his eyes and looked down. He saw Shun sucking hip up with a shower cap on.

He asked her, "What was she doing and where the hell was Punkin?" Shun took his dick out of her mouth and said, "She is in the other shower." Shun then proceeded to finish what she started. Quies was standing there letting the water beat off his body while Shun was sucking him off. As bad as he didn't want to, he knew he had to stop Shun before Punkin caught them.

Shun was making it feel so good, to the point where he didn't want her to stop. Quies turned off the water and told Shun to stop and leave before Punkin saw her. Shun gave Quies the same clothes from last time while she took his outfit to the wash. Shun left his money and gun on the counter. Quies got out of the shower and got dressed.

Quies thought Shun would have tripped but he had forgotten that she told him to bring his gun in. As he came out of the restroom, he saw Punkin and Shun leaning up against the wall. He looked at them with a crazy look, but Punkin and Shun started laughing. Shun told Quies to follow her so she could show him where he would be sleeping. Quies kept hearing them giggle, but he didn't see anything funny.

As they went inside the guest room Punkin pushed up the door and locked it behind her. Quies turned around to see what was going on and Punkin began taking her clothes off. Quies looked around to see where Shun was. He was surprised, Shun was doing the same thing, taking her clothes off too. Shun and Punkin were both naked and approached Quies.

Punkin took Quies' shirt while Shun took off his pants. Punkin began kissing him while Shun finished what she had started earlier in the shower, Quies didn't know what to do.

Even though Quies was shocked he suddenly felt extremely relaxed. Shun and Punkin both got onto the bed on all fours. Quies didn't know who to hit first.

Both of them had nice asses and pretty little pussies. Quies just did what he thought was right, started with Punkin. She was so tight and wet Quies couldn't stand up in it, so he pulled out and slid into Shun. Shun was wet and tight too, but not as much as Punkin. Quies stroked Shun and Shun fingered Punkin.

Once he felt that he was good enough to fuck Punkin he pulled out and began stroking her. Quies thought to himself, "Now I see why that nigga is so crazy about her." Quies felt himself about to cum, so he chilled out for a second and then switched positions. He laid down and let Shun ride him while he ate out Punkin. Quies was getting nutted on both ways.

Punkin was cumming back to back, but she wanted to ride Quies. Punkin made Shun get up and switch with her. She got on top of Quies and slow grinded him. Quies reached around and gripped Punkin on the ass. It was like her ass just melted in his hand, it was so soft.

As she sped up, Quies felt like he was about to cum again. He flipped Shun and Punkin off of him and laid them both on their backs. He went straight into Shun and started tearing that ass up. Punkin told Quies to stop cause she was feeling some type of way. Quies thought it was because he was messing with Shun more than her, but Punkin came out and said, "I'm in love with you Quies, I can't do this anymore."

With an awkward silence in the room, and Shun being her right hand man she told Quies to stop. Quies sat on the bed mad as hell. Now that is Punkin's second time getting Quies hard as hell and not finishing job. He thought to himself. Punkin kissed Quies and told him to put his clothes on.

Shun and Punkin got all of their things and left out of the room. Quies saw some lotion on the dresser, so he grabbed it, locked the door, and finished himself off. He cleaned up and unlocked the door. Now that that was over with, he jumped back in bed and slowly started to drift off to sleep. Just as Quies was about to fall asleep he heard Punkin enter the room and then felt slide into bed with him.

Quies didn't even acknowledge her being in the bed next to him.

The next evening, Quies woke up and Punkin was sitting on the bed just staring at him. He thought he was dreaming until Punkin said something to him about getting up. Quies sat up in the bed and Punkin kissed him. She told him to get dressed cause they were about to leave.

Quies got up and got dressed. As they left Shun's house, Punkin let it be known that Quies was now her man for real. Punkin didn't waste any time getting back to the house. As she walked into the house, she saw all rose petals that Quies had laid out the day before. She followed the roses all the way to the bedroom, where she found a dozen roses sitting on her dresser.

She also noticed Quies had set up the room with candles. Punkin began to cry as she walked into the bathroom to wash her face, where she found a tub full of water and rose petals. Punkin couldn't believe how much Quies went out of his way to do all of this for her. Punkin decided to refill the bathtub with fresh hot water, and lit the candles in the bathroom as well as the ones in the bedroom. Punkin found one of her romantic slow CDs and put it on right in time before Quies walked in.

As he got closer to the room he heard Jagged Edge playing. He noticed that the only light in the house was coming from the candles he had set up the day before. Punkin was sitting in the tub full of bubbles and rose petals. As Quies entered the bathroom, he noticed Punkin in the tub, she told him to get in. Quies did what he was told and got into the tub.

They soaked and talked for about 30 minutes. Quies got tired of it, especially just talking. He took Punkin out of the tub and into the room. Punkin has been waiting on this day so she could show him what she was working with. Quies laid Punkin on the bed and began kissing every part of her body.

Quies wanted to take his time with her because she meant a lot to him, more than anyone else has. He worked his way back up and started giving her oral sex just to start her off. Once he got rock hard he placed himself inside her, taking long soft strokes as he kissed her. Then he began sucking on her breasts as he speeded up. Quies flipped Punkin over and started hitting it from the back.

Each time she came back on him, her ass was smacking his thighs. Her ass was jiggling out of this world. Quies was loving it, he kept grabbing her ass and Punkin became wetter and wetter with each stroke. Quies felt himself about to cum, but he didn't stop. He kept on going until they both climaxed at the same time.

Quies tried to play it off like he hadn't cummed yet, so he kept on stroking. He just snapped and started thinking about all the shit that's been going on about her. Quies started beating that pussy up taking all of his frustration and anger out on it. Quies turned into a porn star on Punkin. They stayed in the house all day having sex.

Quies would only let Punkin use the bathroom and eat then they would go right back to it. They fucked so much throughout the day that they eventually fell asleep like they were fucking, Punkin was laying on Quies like she was riding him.

CHAPTER 9

The next morning Quies woke up to Punkin sucking on him. He was shocked because he wasn't used to waking up to that. He looked down at Punkin and she was looking up at him with those pretty brown eyes bobbing up and down. Then she climbed on top of him and started rotating her hips as she bounced up and down on his rock hard cock. Punkin was so wet and felt so good that Quies didn't last no time at all, he just skeeted all over her.

Punkin got up and told Quies to get ready for work. Quies felt like a piece of meat the way she just fucked him then got up, but at the same time he liked it. Quies knew it was going to be a good day as he got dressed. Once he got dressed, him and Punkin left the house and headed to work. While they were driving, Punkin looked over at Quies and asked him if she could ask him something.

Quies told her to go ahead, she could ask him anything. Punkin proceeded to ask all kinds of questions. She was just making sure that Quies wasn't planning on leaving her. She didn't care about him messing around with other females, due to it being part of his job. She just wanted to make sure that at the end of the day he was hers.

As they pulled up at the shop, Quies turned towards Punkin and said, "Look shawty, I'm fucking with your campaign, so stop worrying about all that other shit". Quies then got out of the car. Punkin loved that Quies had a gangsta side and a sweet side to him, especially because he knew how to turn it on and off. Punkin sat in the car just thinking about Quies for about ten minutes. Once she got out of the car and started walking to the door, Quies pulled around and called Punkin to the van.

When she came over Quies kissed her and then drove off. As he was heading to his designation, out of nowhere he felt a hard impact from behind him hitting the van. He stopped and got out of the van to see if everyone was ok. Little did he know, it was another ambush. Niggas jumped out of an "99" Suburban with Mac11s, AKs, Techs, and M-4s.

Quies eyes got big as hell, and the first thing that came to mind was to run. Quies knew he was about to die, but he ran anyway. As he ran back to the van all he heard was gunshots. Bullets were flying by his head, luckily Quies made it in the van. Bullets started tearing into the van and shredding it into pieces.

He hit the gas trying to get away, but the van barely did 100 mph and Quies was trying to make it do the whole thing. The Suburban kept trying to get on the side of him, but he wouldn't let them pass. Quies took them all down back roads and in places that had a lot of people, but they wouldn't back off. Each time Quies thought they were out of bullets, it rained even more of them. These niggas were hanging out of all the windows as well as the sunroof.

Quies had remembered that he had the F-N in the van, so he reached and pulled it out while still driving and fired back. Quies knew these niggas meant business cause they really wanted him dead. He couldn't think of the last time he had this much beef. Except for Pat, and he was used to him handling his own business so he knew it wasn't him. At least he didn't think it was him.

The Suburban slowed down as Quies fired at it. Quies just kept going trying to get as far away as possible. He maintained a fast pace while keeping one eye on the road and the other on the mirrors.

Quies was all out of ammunition and his only hope is to lose them. But he spoke too soon because the Suburban came flying up behind him, once he stopped shooting.

It was like they went and got more guns and ammunition, because when they came back up on Quies they unloaded a tremendous amount of bullets. They had shot the van up so much until the door was hanging off. Quies ended up on Industrial Blvd. and he was running out of gas. Quies spotted two cop cars sitting at the BP gas station. He knew that this was his only chance of getting away.

He drove by the cop cars at tip speed and as he looked back he saw the flashing lights come on. The cops pulled out to chase him, now he had the cops and the Suburban after him. The guys in the Suburban hung out their window and started shooting at the cops. They flipped the first cop car and caught up with the second one and bumped it from behind. The cop car lost control and then they shot out the gas tank and blew it up.

Quies was trying to figure out why they had done that to him, but he figured they didn't want him that badly. He figured that there isn't anything like killing or shooting a nigga at point blank range. Then he heard a loud boom, and the van began to fishtail. Quies lost complete control and the van flipped on its side and began to slide. As soon as it slowed down, Quies climbed out and began rolling.

Quies finally got up and took off running, he ran to the Travel Lodge which was located right off the highway. This particular spot was known to be a high prostitution area, so he knew he would be able to find a room to duck off into. He ran room to room trying to open everyone.

Soon enough he saw a maid coming out of a room, he pushed

her into the doorway as he ran into the room. The maid started to scream, Quies quickly put his hand over her mouth and explained that he wasn't going to hurt her and to shut the fuck up.

He sat her down on the bed and made sure the blinds were closed. Then he called back to the shop to let Shun and Punkin know what was going on. And that they needed to get a tow truck ASAP for the van. As soon as he hung up the phone, he called T-Mac to see where he was at. Unfortunately he was on the other side of town.

T-Mac said he was going to make a call to his Locs and see if they could handle it for him while he was out. They got off the phone and Quies called Rufus to see what his location was. Because he needed some more ammo, but he told him the same thing that T-Mac said. Quies sat in the room thinking of a plan to get away. An hour had passed and Quies was still sitting there.

He had to pay the maid off because he knew she would rat on him for being in the room and taking up her time. He had to let her go too because she was being called over her radio. As he came out of the room, he heard gunshots going off, so he fell back. Quies waited about five minutes then looked out the window. He saw niggas with blue bandanas and some with black ones shooting it out with each other.

Quies came back out the room and started running. Once he got a better view of things he noticed them niggas, was shooting it out with the Suburban and the cops. Quies turned around and started running the other way. As he ran across the street to get on the bus he heard someone honking the horn at him, but he kept running. As soon as he made it across the street, a gold BMW pulled up on him.

As he leaned down to see who it was he saw Kim sitting in the driver seat. He started smiling from ear to ear as he got into the car.

Kim started asking him all kinds of questions about why he was walking and what he was doing in this type of area. Quies couldn't answer none of her questions because he didn't know how she would react. He just told her to take him somewhere safe, Kim looked at him and pulled out a 40 caliber with an extended clip.

And told Quies that he is always safe with her. Queis knew Kim was crazy, but he didn't know this white chick was gangsta like that. He told her to slowly drive by where they were shooting at so he could see what was going on. She drove close enough so they could see the outcome of everything. But the cops were getting too deep and all of the GD's and Crips had left.

All that was left was those crazy fools that were after him shooting it out with the cops. It looked like the niggas from the Suburban had called for backup. Quies told Kim to drive off and go somewhere they could hide out for a minute. Kim pulled off and turned her radio up, she was listening to some old Pastor Troy, "We Ready". Quies couldn't do anything but laugh cause he realized he had a down ass snow bunny.

While Kim was driving, Quies called back to the shop to let them know that he had gotten away and he was going to hide out for a while. Punkin told Quies that they had the tow-truck put up the van and it was back at the shop. Quies wanted to hang up in her face cause the van was the only thing she could talk about at the time. Quies told Punkin that he was about to go, and he would call her later. Just before Punkin hung up she told Quies she loved him.

Then he called T-Mac and Rufus to tell them thanks for sending their team to help out. Before he knew it they were pulling into Kim's driveway. Just as they were pulling in, Quies received a text from Punkin letting him know that she was going to be staying at

Shun's house. He responded back saying ok and call me later baby. They got out of the car and went inside.

The first thing Quies did was turned on the TV to see if the news was on, but it wasn't 5

O'clock yet. He sat on the couch waiting for the news to come on in ten minutes. When Kimberly sat down next to him, the first thing that came out of her mouth was, "Nigga you owe me, and you know what I want". Quies was startled and didn't know what to say, because she just called him a nigga, and she was bold as she said it.

Quies knew he couldn't act crazy right now cause he needed her.

And on top of that he didn't know where she put the 40cal. at. Quies broke his silence when the news came on. He just told her that he had her just let him check out the news first. As they watched the news, it showed the shoot out the cops and them locking up the guys that were chasing him. One of the guys looked into the camera and made a statement, "We are still coming for you".

Fortunately the cops have no idea who he is talking about, but Quies sure did. The news reporter said they have an eyewitness, Quies' heart dropped. He was hoping that it wasn't the maid that he had in the room.Right before they were going to show the witness they went to commercial. Quies was pissed cause he really wanted to see who it was and what they had to say.

He had made a vow that he wasn't going back to prison, they would have to kill him before he let them get to him. Kim looked at Quies and told him to let her help take his mind off all of this. Quies didn't fell like fucking at the time, his mind was on getting out of this bullshit.

He knew the only way was to kill Pat cause he was calling all the shots, but right now shit was too hot in the streets. Kim didn't care that Quies had other things on his mind, she unbuckled his pants and pulled out his dick and began to suck it.

Quies started feeling better, the way Kim was sucking and playing with his balls. He almost forgot about him being shot at. The news came back on, Quies moved Kim out of the way so he could focus on what they were saying. As they showed the witness, Quies became even more relaxed cause it wasn't the maid. The witness happened to be some guy just talking about the shooting and how all the gang members came out of nowhere and targeted the Suburban.

As the news went on talking about what was going on, breaking news shot across the TV. "This just in; all of this is somehow tied in from the other night in Centennial Park." They showed the video clips again and Quies got nervous all over. The news reporter stated that they still didn't have any name for the other suspect or what he looked like.

Quies didn't know how many niggas Pat had done sent after him, so he still had to lay low.

He turned off the TV and grabbed Kim by her head and pushed it in his lap. Not giving her the opportunity to say or ask anything, he just filled her mouth with his cock. Kim started sucking until Quies became rock hard. Kim got up and turned her back towards Quies and sat in his lap. Kim then placed Quies inside of her and grabbed her ankles while bouncing up and down on him.

Each time she came up on his dick she squeezed her kitty muscle and looked back at Quies. Quies grabbed her ass and bounced her up and down as hard as he could. Kim started squirting cum all on him as she squirmed to get out of that position.

Quies held her by her hips and rammed himself in her harder

and harder. The harder he got the more she came and tried to wiggle away.

She then got into a handstand position so she could do the 69 position. Quies ate her for a few minutes but really wasn't feeling it, he really wanted to beat that kitty up. He flipped Kim back over and took her up stairs. As they got in the room they both got undressed and picked up where they left off. Quies laid on the bed so she could ride him, and before she startled him, she pulled out one of her toys.

She said don't worry it's not for you because it was a vibrating strap-on. While her toy vibrated on her clitoris, she slowly rode Quies up and down and rotated her hips in a grinding motion. As she grinded and bounced all on Quies, out of nowhere his cell phone began to ring. Kim stopped and got up to grab his pants and handed them to him. Quies pulled out his phone to see who it was.

When he looked at his phone he thought to himself, "she would call at this time." Quies sat the phone down and went back to caressing Kim. Kim didn't say anything, she just looked at him. Then his phone started ringing again and Kim told him to just answer it. As he answered the phone, Kim heard Punkin's voice on the other end.

She gave Quies a strange look, then began to ride and grind on him extra hard as she put her nails into his chest. Quies couldn't even talk to Punkin like he needed or wanted too. Kim was riding him so good until Quies' toes started curling and he began climaxing. Quies caught himself about to moan as he came, so he hung up on Punkin. She called right back, but Quies didn't answer.

Punkin called right back, Kim looked at Quies again with another but stranger look and jumped off of him and ran to the bathroom. Quies hurried and answered the phone before it stopped ringing, and before Punkin could say anything, Quies apologized for hanging up. Punkin asked him where he was and how long was he going to stay away from her. Quies told Punkin that he couldn't answer that question, but just know that he was safe.

Kim came out of the bathroom crying. Quies looked up and told Punkin that he would call her back in two minutes. As he hung up the phone he walked over to Kim to find out what was wrong. Kim started crying louder as she told Quies that he was cheating on her. Quies explained to Kim that he didn't even know that they were together and he was just doing his job all the times they had sex.

This happened to be the first time they did it and she didn't pay. Kim got mad and jumped up and grabbed a shoe box and pulled out stacks of money. Then threw it at Quies, yelling at him that if it's the money you want, here it is. He looked at all the money and thought about taking it and leaving Kim's crazy ass, but it wasn't about the money with him, even though he could use it. Quies' heart was with Punkin, but now he owed Kim a favor because she saved his ass.

Quies started thinking about all the shit that is going on right now. He has two chicks that want to be with him right now and niggas who are out to kill him. His situation is getting worse by the minute. Each one of the chicks were in love with him and were willing to take care of him too. Quies knew that he could find away to make the girls happy, but he just had to find away to get these niggas off his back.

Quies got up and told Kim that he would be right back. As he walked out the door he got his phone so he could call Punkin back. Quies stood on the outside of the door as he talked to Punkin, letting her know that he was going to be hiding out for a while. And he needed her to go along with her every day schedule. If those niggas were watching her they wouldn't see him and things could cool down for awhile and then he would pop back up.

Punkin started crying because she thought it was over for them. Quies told her that he still loved her and they were still together. He just wanted to get a plan together so he wouldn't lose her for good with all the bullshit that's been going on. Quies hung up the phone and would call her later. As he walked back in the room, Kim had the gun aimed at her head.

He yelled at her to put the gun down cause he wasn't going anywhere. Kim looked up and told Quies to promise her that he wasn't going to leave her. He slowly walked over to the bed and promised her that he wasn't going to leave. Then he began kissing her to relax her so he could take the gun out of her hand. He eased the gun out of her hand and quickly jumped back and broke the gun down.

He then went fussing at her for putting the gun to her head and threatening to kill herself. Quies told her if she killed herself they couldn't be together. Kim immediately got happy and jumped off the bed into his arms. Quies knew that this was going to be a hard job dealing with Kim. He needed something too hard to drink, cause it was going to be a long night.

He asked Kim if she had any liquor, she told him that she had this new liquor which hasn't even come out yet. Quies walked down stairs into the kitchen to look for the liquor. But it wasn't in the refrigerator so he asked Kim where it was. Kim said that it was in the pantry, so he went to the pantry and saw two cases of ADIA. He opened up a box and grabbed a bottle to fix him a glass.

As he made his way back up stairs he sipped on his drink and it had a smooth taste as it went down. Before he knew it, it was all gone, so he just grabbed the bottle. When he got to the room he sipped on the ADIA until he started feeling the buzz kick in and he started feeling himself. He looked at Kim and started spitting game that he didn't even know he had. As he made his way to Kim, she began to turn red cause she never seen him like this, he was talking so smooth and sexy to her.

Quies reached Kim and began kissing her until he got hard, then made love to her for hours. The more slippery she got the longer he went, Kim was falling deeper in love with Quies. They made love and hot sweaty sex until daybreak

CHAPTER 10

The next evening, Quies woke up to the sweet smell of syrup, and music,blaring through the speakers. Quies got out the bed and went right to the bathroom to take his morning piss and freshen up. He made his way down stairs to the kitchen to see Kim cooking away as she listened to "You Changed Me", by Jamie Fox and Chris Brown. Quies crept up on Kim and wrapped his arms around her and began kissing on her neck. Kim started melting in his arms while he was kissing her.

She turned around and wrapped her arms around his neck and kissed him good morning then told him to set the table. As he set the table, Kim walked over with the plates, she had breakfast and lunch all on one plate. Quies thought he was at IHOP or somewhere with all that food. As they sat down to eat, Kim asked Quies if he needed to go anywhere today or he wanted to do anything.

The first thing that came to his mind was going to see Punkin, and to make some type of plans to get rid of that nigga Pat. He told Kim yea, he needed to make a few runs. But he didn't know if she was going to try and tag along. Once they finished eating, Kim gave Quies the keys to the car and a stack of money. Quies knew he could get used to this lifestyle.

As he left the house, Kim pulled out behind him in her other car. Quies just pulled off as if he was up to nothing and didn't care if she followed him. As he made his way up the road on to the expressway, Kim kept going straight ahead. That was Quies' clue to hit the gas.

He pulled out his phone and sent a text to Punkin to see where she was at. She called right back.

"Hello"

"Hey Baby, I miss you so much", Punkin said. "Yo baby, where you at?"

"I'm at work baby, you know that."

"Ok, but has anybody been around the shop?"

"No, I haven't seen anyone, and it's just me and Shun like always". "Ok baby, just keep your eyes open and I'll call you later."

As Quies was hanging up the phone he was pulling up at the shop. Before he got out of the car, he looked around to see if anything looked suspicious. He then got out of the car and walked into the shop. As he walked in, Punkin began to ask him if he needed help. But as she turned around she saw it was Quies and got excited.

Punkin ran around the desk and jumped into Quies' arms kissing and hugging him. Quies told Punkin to call Shun up front to watch the desk while he talked to her in the back. Punkin grabbed the phone and called for Shun. As Shun walked up front, she had a huge smile on her face when she noticed Quies. "I'm glad to see that you're ok Quies,"

"Yeah me too, but I'm not going to be able to stay up here long," Quies responded.

Punkin and Shun both said, "Why?"

"I have to continue to lay low for the time being, I just came by to see Punkin and to get some things out of the van."

"Oh ok, well the van is in the back and you're just in time because they are coming by sometime today to get it."

"Who's coming to get the van?"

"The insurance company crazy."

As they went to the back, Punkin couldn't stop looking at Quies. He knew what that look meant, but he played it cool until he got everything out of the van. Once he got his F-N from under the seat, he looked around to see if there was anything else he needed. He spotted the glass bottle of acid untouched, he grabbed it and set it on the outside of the van. Punkin looked at it, then asked him where did that come from.

Quies just responded not to worry about it, just act like you never saw it. Punkin just shook her head and asked how long he thought he was going to be away for. Quies didn't really know so he just shook his head and told her that he was working on some things. Quies just looked at Pun kin and realized the more he looked at her the more he missed her. Quies grabbed Pun kin and snatched her pants down, bent her over, and went up in her.

With each stroke he did it harder and harder with more force. He gripped her by her neck and pulled her back to him and told her that she better not give his pussy away, then kissed her as he nutted all in her. When they finished they pulled up their pants. Quies looked Punkin in the eyes and told her that he loved her. Punkin smiled and told him that she loved him too and she couldn't wait for all this to be over.

Quies picked up the bottle of acid and walked back to the front. Shun was standing there laughing at them, but they didn't know what she was laughing at. Quies kissed Punkin and walked out the door and he heard Shun yell out see you later minute man. Quies laughed to himself as the door shut. He put the acid in the trunk and as he was letting the trunk down he saw a green cutlass ride by and slow down just a little.

Quies hurried and got into the car before anybody noticed him.

He didn't know what kind of cars Pat had or if that was anybody with him. He just wanted to stay under the radar for as long as possible. Driving off Quies watched his back to make sure that the Cutlass was not following him, but it wasn't anywhere in sight. As he got down the street, he pulled into a Pawn Shop parking lot and parked the car.

He put the F-N under the seat so no one would think he was going to rob them. He locked up the car and went inside. He didn't waste any time and went right to the bullets and asked for six boxes. Quies knew it looked crazy for him to buy all of that at once but he really didn't have any other choice due to the situation he was in. He figured that it was better to have enough ammo than not to have enough.

If anyone decided to ask what he was going to do with all that ammo, he just was going to say he was going to gun range for target practice. Approaching the checkout counter, Quies asked one of the employees to get him an extra clip for a F-N. They brought the clip back and checked Quies out, they didn't even ask any questions. Quies grabbed his bag and told the guy to have a nice day and left. As he got in the car, he locked the doors and got the F-N from under the seat and loaded up both the clips.

Once the clips were loaded he pulled out of the parking lot and headed straight to the eastside. It dawned on him that he left his T.O. Green and Fly Da Bandit mixtapes in the van. He called Punkin and told her to go grab them and put them up for him. Arriving at McDonald's, Quies put the F-N on his hip and got out of the car. He looked around and checked out his surroundings, he didn't want to get caught slipping.

Walking into the McDonald's all eyes were on him. Quies asked if Angel was in as he ordered a McChicken with a large coke. As he waited for his order, Angel came walking towards him.

"Hey stranger."

"What's up cutie, how have you been since the last time we talked?" "I'm good, just the same ol same ol."

"Oh that's what's up, hey you have a few minutes so we could talk?" "Yeah sure"

Quies got his order and they went to a table so they could talk. They sat at the table and talked for an hour before Angel realized she had to get back to work. Quies knew if he got in good with her he could get closer to Pat to make his move. Angel got up to head back to work and before she got too far off Quies pulled her hand to get her attention. As she turned around he asked for her number, but she shut him down and told him that she had a man.

Angel walked off and Quies watched her as he thought to himself, "Dam I got to get her." That was his only way to find out what all Pat got going on, and who he was plugged in with. Leaving McDonald's, Quies knew that it would take a minute for Angel to give him her number because Pat was crazy and he knew that first hand. He got in the car and drove off. The whole time he was driving back to Kim's house he was thinking of a plan to get Angel on his side.

Pulling up in the driveway, he noticed that Kimberly was back. He parked the car and went in the house to see that Kim had decorated the house for a romantic evening. He walked around the house to find her, she was laying in the closet on bags of clothes. Quies picked her up and took her to the bed and laid her down. He went back to the closet and started going through all the bags and it wasn't anything but designer clothes for men.

Before he could finish going through the bags Kim came and stood in the doorway and cleared her throat. Quies jumped as he got caught being nosey, he stood up to ask Kim who all those clothes were for. Kim told him that was for her King, the Messiah of her life. From that moment on Quies knew that Kim would try to kill him if he tried to leave her. So he had to watch what he did or what he said to her, but at the same time Quies felt that this could be what's best.

Quies jumped up and kissed Kim to show that he was thankful for all his gifts, then Kim asked him where he was. Quies got quiet and looked at her with a puzzled look. Kim smiled and told him she was just playing as she walked away from the doorway. Quies got up and chased Kim around the room until he caught up with her. He then laid her on the bed.

The romantically wrestled and rolled around on the bed, then they began to passionately kiss one another. Which in time led them to making unconditional love. Two hours had passed and Kim got up to fix dinner. While Kim was fixing dinner Quies was on the phone with Punkin. He made sure that she was ok and that nothing out of the ordinary happened today while she was at work.

The only thing that she kept talking about was how she missed him and wanted some good loving. Quies had to pull out his C game to keep both chicks happy, cause they were already crazy about him. The only thing that was on his mind was if they ever bumped heads, what would happen. He didn't want Kim to shoot Punkin. Kim yelled up stairs for Quies to come eat, so he got off the phone.

Quies came downstairs and Kim had candles lit and some soft jazz playing with champagne on the table. He sat down as she brought the plate to the table. She had cooked a five star meal, Quies was surprised that she cooked like she did. He was just hoping that it tasted as good as it looked and smelled. Kim sat down and Quies dug in, he didn't waste any time or wait for her to say Grace, or anything for that.

Kim just looked at him and began eating herself. Once they finished eating Quies did the dishes while Kim took a shower. He texted Punkin and told her that he will see her tomorrow if he could, he then turned his phone off and went to get into the shower with Kim. Kim started washing his back then worked her way to the front of his body. Gently washing his balls, Quies told Kim she better stop before she starts something.

That was all she wanted to hear. She dropped her rag, bent over with her ass in front of Quies, and backed it up for him to put himself inside her. Quies smacked her on the ass and told her that she was a freak as he went up inside her. Kim started out slowly bouncing back and forward to find her groove, while Quies just stood behind her. Then she grabbed the soap holder on the wall and went faster.

Quies didn't know if it was the water that made her this wet because this was the wettest she has ever been, dripping.

Quies grabbed her by her hips and went even faster feeling himself about to climax, he pulled her closer as he released himself in her. After he was finished, they finished washing up and got out of the shower. As they dried off, Quies looked at Kim and realized he was really starting to like her. As they left the bathroom, Kim looked back at Quies and told him that she had a big day tomorrow and she needed some sleep.

Quies got in bed and turned the TV on until he fell asleep. The next day Quies woke up to an empty bed, he got up and got himself together so he could start his day. As he left the house, he turned on his phone and he had a message. He didn't check it because he thought it was Punkin and that's where he was headed. Getting on the highway he thought about going to see Angel too.

So she could give in and just give him her number. Quies really wanted to fuck Angel any way cause she was a bad chick, but he didn't want to mix business with pleasure.

Coming up on his exit, he noticed that he needed some gas. And the only gas station was there was QT, so he pulled up to fill the tank. As he was walking inside the store he saw the green cutlass four pumps down.

But he never saw who was in it that day it drove by the shop and as he opened the door a guy walked out yelling at someone. The only thing he caught was "Girl you better hurry up, you know Pat gone be mad if we get there late to visit him." Quies went into his thinking mood and started clutching on the F-N that he kept on his hip. Once he was all the way in store he looked around before he walked any farther and there was Angel. She looked even better in street clothes than her work uniform.

The way her jeans fitted and the open toe high heels set the whole outfit off. She turned around to see Quies admiring her, she smiled as she spoke as if she was happy to see him. Quies spoke back, then asked where she was headed to, to see if that guy was talking to her. Angel dropped her head as if she was ashamed to tell him she was going to see her man. Angel told him anyways, and Quies felt a little relaxed to know Pat was locked up.

Quies paid for his gas and told her to give him her number, so if she ever got lonely they could go out on a little respectable date. Angel thought about it, then she gave him her number and walked out. Quies saw his plan coming together, he just had to play his cards right and get in real good with her. While he was pumping his gas, he became really hungry and figured he would take Punkin out to eat for lunch. He filled the tank and hopped in the car and pulled off.

As he arrived at the shop Punkin was standing outside, he parked the car and got out. Punkin saw him and ran to the car. She was not used to him not being at home with her. Quies told her to call Shun and tell her you are about to leave to get something to eat with me and you'll be back. Quies didn't wait for Shun to say yes or no, he just pulled off.

He took her to Lupoe's Sports and Grill, located on the Southside of Atlanta. It was the newest and hottest restaurant that just opened. As they sat down, Quies told the waitress to bring them the best of everything they had from appetizers to desserts, they wanted the best. Punkin looked shocked how Quies was handling things. They sat back and kicked it while they waited on their food.

Hours had passed and they were still eating and talking. Quies took Punkin's mind far off of work, but Shun started blowing up her phone, so they had to leave. They got her a meal to go so she wouldn't be at Punkin. Once they got back on the road, Quies did a hundred mph trying to get her back. Pulling up at the shop, he dropped Punkin off at the door.

Shun came out cursing them both out then turned around and told Quies he needed to bring his ass back to work. She was missing out on a lot of money because he had a lot of repeat customers that were looking for him. And they had referred him to others. Quies told Shun that he would be back just give him a minute to work something out, then drove off. As he made his way down the road, he thought about all the nice things Kim had bought him the other day.

He decided to stop and get her a little something with the money she gave him. He knew he had to stay on her good side while he was in the house. As he went down the street he hit little outlet stores to pick up her some clothes and jewelry with a thing of flowers. After he got done shopping he went right to the house. As he pulled into the driveway he noticed that Kim wasn't even home yet, so he parked the car and unloaded it.

He took all of her things upstairs and put them in the closet to surprise her when she came home. Quies turned on the TV to enjoy the 75inc plasma they had in the bedroom. Quies flipped through the channels and came across one of his favorite movies, "Friday After Next". He jumped up and ran downstairs to fix him a bite to eat and grabbed the whole bottle of ADIA, then went back upstairs. As he watched the movies he ate and drank until he passed out.

CHAPTER 11

Three months later Quies felt as if he was on top of the world. He had three chicks that he was juggling around and he became the head maintenance man at Paradise Maintenance Service. And he had Angel wrapped around his finger, so he knew Pat's every move. Even though he was still locked up. Trying not to become tender dick with Angel because it was just all business with them but she didn't know it.

Quies hated that he had to treat such a beautiful chick like that but that was the only way he stayed a step ahead. Quies laid in the bed thinking to him after been woke up by Kim running back and forward to the bathroom throwing up. He rolled over to see what time it was. It was that time already. Quies got out the bed to get ready for work, and Kim was sitting on the floor hugging the toilet.

He checked on her but she pushed him away as she grabbed the toilet for another round. He left and went on his way and got in the car. He turned on the phone and as it powered up. It made a beeping sound to notify him that he had 5 new messages. He checked his messages as he headed to work and they all were from Punkin.

But she didn't really say anything but call her, so Quies didn't pay it any attention since he was on his way to work anyways. 30 minutes later he pulled up at the job and the parking lot was full but all the vans were gone. As he walked on the inside he saw Shun sitting behind the receptionist desk, he asked her where was Punkin? Shun looked at him and smiled then told him she gave her the day off because she had morning sickness. Quies gave Shun a crazy look then just shook his head.

As he walked to the back to get his van, Shun yelled out at him "yeah you about to be a daddy". He didn't even bother to look back; the thought of him becoming a dad had his mind in another world. As he got into the van he called up Punkin to see what was really going on. "Hello"

"Yo what's up boo? I saw where you left them messages." "Yea, I just want you to know that I'm having your baby"

"What?! Are you for real?" "Yea Quies I'm ...."

"Aye hold that thought someone on my other line. "Yo what's up Kim" "Damn nigga that's how you talk to your baby momma?"

"What? My baby momma what are you talking about?" "Quies I am pregnant with your baby."

"Ok we gonna talk when I get home" Quies said as he cleared the line with Kim and clicked back over to Punkin.

"Yo Punkin"

"Yea, bae I'm here."

"So you having my baby, well look we gonna have to talk later about this."

As Quies got off the phone with Punkin he felt like the world just came falling down on him. And the only thing he was hoping now was that Angel didn't call and said she was pregnant too. He knew it was gone be some shit behind all of this once Kim and Punkin both found out that they are pregnant by him. As he arrived at his first job for the day he knew that he wasn't going to be able to perform his best on whatever the job was. Walking inside the house he noticed that the house was a home base day care.

And he got even drunker than he was, all the little kids were running around. He walked farther into the house to see a nice looking older lady talking on the phone. As he approached her he saw pictures of Pat hanging on the wall. His heart dropped because he thought he was being set up, and he had bone left the 44 in the van.

As he turned around to leave back out the house before the lady said anything or noticed him, she was hanging up the phone. "Hey handsome, how may I help you?"

"Umm .... Yes ma'am you can, I had a work order for this address." "Oh yeah baby right this way the kitchen sink won't stop running."

As they walked to the kitchen, Quies couldn't stop thinking that he was being set up. The lady pointed to the slink and Quies walked over to check it out. He turned around and told the lady that it was a small problem and it wouldn't take any time for him to fix it. Quies went back out to the van to grab the 44 and the other tools that he needed, and went back inside. Walking back in the kitchen Quies got his eyes full.

The lady had gone and got undressed the only thing she had on was her panties and bra. She was bent over looking in the bottom cabinet, and her pussy was so fat it was hanging out of her panties. Quies walked over and started fixing on the sink; Pattie came over to him and stuck her hand down his pants. She felt the 44 and removed her hand then looked at him and said "Damn baby I didn't know you was packing I just wanted to give yo fine ass a tip".

Quies quickly fixed the slink and once he turned around Pattie tried it again. But this time she pulled his pants down. Quies went to fumbling around trying to catch the pistol before it hit the ground. As he caught the pistol he stood back up and Ms.Pattie went to sucking on his cock. Quies could tell that she was a pro; she was sucking on his cock so good it was like she was trying to put a hickey on his dick head.

Quies couldn't help himself; he released all in her mouth and on her face. And as he opened his eyes he saw a baby standing in the doorway with a bottle in his mouth. He pulled up his pants and grabbed his pistol and tools and ran out the door. As he got in the van he realized why Pat was so fucked up. His mom was a freak and she didn't care what she did or who she did it with.

As he drove down the road his phone went off, it was Angel. The first thing came to his mind was this bicth is pregnant too and calling to let me know. He answered the phone and Angel first words were baby I got to tell you something. Quies replied with a little bit of an attitude "what you pregnant." Angel laughed and said no but Pat will be coming home soon and you are what I want before he gets out.

He laughed as he told her ok I'll be over later then hung up the phone. Getting on the highway he spotted the green Cutlass headed in the direction he had just came from. Quies got back on the phone to call Angel to see if she had heard anything about Pat getting out early or anything. But she didn't pick up the phone. Quies called Shun and told her that he had some serious business that he needed to handle and needed the rest of the day off.

As he headed back to the shop he called Punkin and told her to get dressed. Then called Kim and told her that he would be home soon and that he was bringing company to the house.

Once he pulled up at the shop he parked the van and jumped in the car. Before he could pull off

Shun yelled out at him "Just because you got some good dick

don't mean you run shit." Quies just kept on driving, as he took the 44 off his hip and placed it under the seat.

Wasting no time, Quies had made it to Punkin's house. He called her and told her to come on out the door. While he was waiting on Punkin to come out the house Angel called.

"Yo what's up"

"Nothing just calling you back I thought you was on your way."

"Yea I'm coming I'm just at work right now." Aye have you heard anything about Pat?" "No not no more then what I told you, why what's up?"

"Oh just checking"

As Punkin gets in the car Quies hangs up the phone then pulls off. Punkin was so excited to the point that she couldn't stop talking. She talked to Quies the whole time until they arrived at Kim's house. As they got out of the car he told Punkin not to say anything, just let him do all the talking. Walking into the house Quies called for Kim and she came running down the stairs until she saw Punkin standing in the lobby of the house.

She slowly walked down as she was looking at Punkin then looked back at Quies. "Girl bring yo ass on down them dam steps" Quies shouted out. Kim came on down and he introduced them to each other. Then took the both to the living room and sat them down. As he explained that they both were pregnant and they had to work something out right now.

Kim and Punkin both didn't want anything to do with each other. Quies looked at them both and out of nowhere he drew his hand back and slapped the shit out of both of them. And told them that they were going to be one big family whether they like it or not.

But then he quickly thought about what he was doing. He knew he couldn't force them into nothing they didn't want to do.

He just knew that he had to go with his "A" game and mix it with a little pimping, that he learned from a nigga name Pimp while he was locked. He began working his game and they were falling for it. Quies tried to see how far he could go with them and before he knew it they grabbed him by both hands and took him up stairs. Entering into the bedroom Kim and Punkin started undressing him as they kissed all parts of his body. Then laid him on the bed and put on a little show for him.

As they undressed each other they throw articles of clothes at him to keep him entertained. Then slowly walked over and got in bed with him. Punkin passed the first kiss to Kim and Kim took over. She began tonguing Punkin down and working her way down her body. Quies sat back to watch Kim do her thing, he knew Punkin would do her thing in a three some but he didn't know Kim would take over like she did.

As she went down on Punkin and gave her oral sex, she took her hand and begun jacking and massaging Quies penis, until he got hard. Then her and Punkin took turns giving him head. Kim got up and ran to the closet, Quies stopped Punkin so he could get up. But before he could get all the way up Kim was on her way back to the bed with something in her hand. Kim looked at Quies and asked him "what was he doing up".

Quies replied "Hell I wanted to know where you were running off to"

"I just went to go get a toy for us daddy, Kim said as they walked back to the bed. But the whole time Quies thought Kim was going to get her gun. As they got back in the bed Quies laid down and

Punkin started back sucking him with her ass in his face. Kim came over and sat on Quies face while she played in Punkin's pussy. Quies ate Kim until she came in his mouth and he felt Punkin nutt dripping on his chest and stomach.

He got up and laid Kim on her back then made Punkin get on top of her in the doggy style. He went back and forth from Punkin to Kim pounding on their kitty making them climax back to back. Then he took Punkin and lay her on her side. And left one leg up and started drilling her while he played with the toy inside of Kim. Quies went on for hours going back and forth between them.

Putting them in all types of position until they all fell asleep. Two hours later Quies woke up from the buzzing sound of his phone. As he got up to answer his phone he made sure that he didn't move too much, because he didn't want to wake up Kim and Punkin. Picking up his phone he walked out the rooms he could talk.

"Damn Quies you just gonna stand a bicth up like that?!"

"Nawl baby I just had to handle a few things but I'm on my way now." "Ok, just call me when you outside."

Quies hangs up the phone and quickly gets dressed. As he heads out the door he stops by the kitchen to grab a bottle of ADIA to take with him. On the way to Angel's house Quies pop the top on the bottle and take a few good drinks. So he would be ready when he got there. As he got closer to the house he started getting a bad feeling about things.

He didn't know if it was the liquor playing with him or what. As he pulled up at the house he parked next door at the empty house. Then called Angel to let her know that he was outside and about to come through the back like he always does. Before he got the car he reached under the seat to grab the 44 revolver and picked up the liquor out of the console then locked the doors. As he put the pistol on his hip he took another hit of the bottle.

Walking to the back of the house Quies thought he heard someone talking, so he looked around but he didn't see anyone. Quies hurried and went inside of the house, where he saw Angel standing about five feet from the patio door. Dressed for a long night of love making and hard sex. Quies came inside the house and set the liquor on the table then shut and locked the patio door behind him.

"Hey baby, I see you brought us something to drink on."

"Yea boo, this some new shit called ADIA" gone fix you a cup while I check the house. "Quies ain't nobody here, you so damn crazy"

While Quies searched the house he noticed in the bedroom that Angel had an AK-47 sitting in the corner by the bed. He walked back to the living room to question Angel. But before he made it out the room she was coming in with the bottle in her hand.

"Yo who shit this is?!"

"Baby that's one of Pat's guns that he keeps over here."

"Well what's it doing pulled out, you ain't never had it out before"

"I know boo but some niggas tried to break in today, that's why I had it out."

"Bicth that better be the reason why it's out, cause if I find out you trying to set me up I'm gonna kill you and whoever."

"Damn baby you just gonna talk to me like that? Quies you know I love you, I wouldn't do that to you."

"Ok if you say so, but for now I need you to come make me happy"

Angel took another drink from the bottle then sat it on the

dresser. As she strutted her way over to Quies, he began taking off his clothes. Angel straddled Quies and wrapped her arms around his neck and started kissing on him. Quies felt himself beginning to rise, he reached down and pulled her panties to the side and placed himself inside of her. Angel grinds on him until he was fully erected.

Then began bouncing up and down while Quies gripped her ass. Quies stood up then laid Angel on her back not missing a stroke, he grinded on her while he stroked and hit them corners. The deeper and harder he got the tighter she squeezed his neck. Quies started going faster and Angel got wetter, she was squirting cum out like it wasn't nothing. He flipped her over on her side and put both of her legs together then banged her kitty vigorously.

He pulled out and went down and started licking and sucking on her wet pussy. Angel grabbed Quies by his ears as he ate her out, the alcohol was kicking in and Angel got even looser. Quies opened her legs back up then put her in the buck, and slowly stroked her insides as she mourned and told him how much she loved him. Quies went from slow and deep to fast and hard. He grabbed Angel by her neck and the faster he went the tighter he got around her neck.

The pussy got wetter. It felt like someone poured a bucket of water on him.

Quies noticed that two hours had passed and he was still standing strong, the alcohol had made him harder than Superman's knee cap. He grabbed Angel and placed her on top of him, letting her ride him. Each time she came up she squeezed her kitty muscles and sprinkled cum all down his shaft.

He pulled her in close to him and then began stabbing her extra fast with his cock. Angel laid her head on his chest as she gripped the sheet while he was hammering on her pussy. Quies pulled out and made Angel give him some head, and then he grabbed her by her hips and lifted her up so he could eat and play with her pussy. Quies was licking on her clitoris as he stuck his tongue inside of her then blew inside her kitty and quickly sucked the air back out.

Angel stops giving him head and looked back at him, because she ain't never felt anything like it. Quies got up and grabbed her to put her in the doggy style position. Then ran to the bathroom and looked in the medicine cabinet to get an alka-seltzer. As he walked back to the bed he broke a small piece off. Then smack Angel on her ass while she looked back at him.

Then he dropped down on his knees and ate her pussy to keep her wet. And came up to eat her ass and slowly worked the little piece of alka-seltzer into her ass. Then slid right back inside of her, as she consumed the alka-seltzer the bubbles made her extra sensitive. Each stroke he took her pussy spited cum out at him. Quies gripped and smacked her ass each time she threw it back at him.

The wetter she got the harder and faster he went. The soft sexy sound of Angel's morn made him melt, as she squinted her eyes from the impact of Quies thrusting himself inside of her. Looking back to mourn, I love you. He grabbed Angel tighter and pulled her closer as he reached his climax. Then he walked to the dresser to get the bottle of ADIA' and took a few sips then laid back on the bed to let his body rejuvenate.

But before he could get comfortable the bedroom door busted open. And Pat was standing in the door way yelling back at his crew "That nigga in here yall!" as he reached for the pistol on his hip. Quies rolled off the bed and grabbed the AK. Then cocked it back and let it rip. Pat shot back as he ran out the room trying not to get shot. Quies heard Angel screaming at the top of her lungs as he chased after Pat.

Chasing him back into the living room where his goons were waiting for him to come around the corner. Quies stopped and stuck the chopper around the corner squeezed the trigger. Pat and the crew returned fire, bullets were flying everywhere. The only thing that was saving Quies was the wall he was hiding+q a behind. He hit the floor and crawled away from the wall so he could see where everybody was at.

There were too many bullets flying in the air for him to stand up and he was out number. Quies knew that he had to use his head to bet them. He counted to three and then stood up and took off running to the first room with a window. He let up the window then jumped out of it. Just so happen the window landed him in the backyard, he could still hear the gun fire as he ran across the yard.

Creeping up to the patio where the glass was broken out from all the bullets. Pat and his crew had finally stopped shooting and made their way to the back of the house. Quies slowly walked in making sure he didn't make any noise for anyone to turn around. Once he noticed that all of them were walking down the hallway, he aimed the chopper in their direction. Before he could fire off around one of the goons turned back, Quies immediately started walking backwards as he let the chopper go.

Body started hitting the ground as they exchanged gunfire. Pat took off running into the bedroom where Angel was hiding from all of the flying bullets. Quies ran back out the patio and ran around to the front of the house. He looked at his car and thought about making a run for it but all of his clothes were still on the inside. He ran to the bedroom window and sent a few shots in the room.

Then he took off and ran back in the house. The only thing on his mind was to kill Pat. As he ran back in the house he picked up a carbon 15 off the floor and kicked Angel's bedroom door in. Not hasting Quies let both guns rip, not caring about nothing he shot up the room. Hoping that he hit and killed Pat.

As he dropped the guns on the floor. And he walked in the room to get his things and to check everything out. Pat rushed full force at him; Quies froze as his life flashed before his eyes. All he could think was this big nigga is about to kill me. Both guns were empty and the only chance he had was to make it to the revolver.

Pat hit Quies with a mean left; waking him out of his daze. Quies stumbled and fell against the wall and Pat kept hitting him trying to break him down. Angel came from under the bed begging Pat to stop. As he threw his next punch Quies ducked and ran to his jeans. Pulling out the 44; he took two shots, one hit the wall and the other hit Pat in the chest.

Pat hit the wall and ran ok out the bedroom door; Quies took another shot and hit him in his leg. Pat fell to the floor half way in the hallway. Quies walked up and stood over him and shot Pat point blank range in the head. Then he turned around and told Angel to help him pull all the bodies into the room. As they dragged the bodies into the room one of Pat's goons wasn't dead.

He rolled over and shot Quies in the shoulder. Quies dropped to the ground and hid behind one of the dead bodies. He took his pistol and hung it over the body and shot two times. Finishing him off he stood up and blood was running down his arm. He made Angel wrap his arm up.

And as soon as she got done Quies looked at her then shot her

Johnques Lupoe

in the chest. He told her he was sorry but he had to do it as he laid her on the floor. He quickly ran and put on his clothes.

As he was leaving out the door he thought the raffles that he had done touched. He turned back to get them and ran to the car.

As he popped the trunk he saw the gallon bottle of acid that he stole a while back. He sat the A-K and Carbon in the trunk and grabbed the bottle. Quies ran back in the house and stopped by the kitchen to find a pair of rubber oven gloves. Putting the gloves on as he walked back to the bedroom, he unscrewed the top and slowly poured the acid on the bodies. The bodies started decapitating instantly.

He made sure he used every drop to cover each body then took the bottle with him. As he walked back to the kitchen, he turned on the gas in the oven. As the gas filled the air of the house Quies began setting things on fire. As the fire began to spared Quies got the bottle and ran to the car. He put the bottle in the trunk and shut it up as he jumped in the car and hauled ass.

As he made it to the end of the road he saw a big fire in his rearview mirror, He hit the gas and didn't look back no more.

CHAPTER 12

Meanwhile back at the house Punkin and Kim were getting to know each other a little bit better. They had come to realize that they both really loved Quies and would do anything to keep him around. Kim and Punkin started coming up with plans and baby names for the kids.

Then it dawn on them that Quies wasn't at the house and it was three o'clock in the morning. He had been gone for about eight hours that they knew of.

And he couldn't say that he was over either of their houses. Punkin got her phone and speed dialed Quies number. The phone just rang and rang. As soon as Punkin hung up Kim tried and the phone did the same thing. They both got up to check outside for the car and Quies was parked in the driveway.

The lights and car were still running. Kim busted out the front door and Punkin followed right behind her. As they got to the car Quies was passed out on the steering wheel. Kim opened the car, they both pulled him out, and took him inside the house. He woke up from all the screaming and crying that they were doing.

But he had lost a lot of blood and he smelled like smoke, Quies ended up passing right back out. Punkin started undressing him to see where all the blood had done came from. The patch work that Angel did before she died was soaked in blood. The liquor had thinned his blood out and his heart rate was up. Kim got on the phone to call the cops for an ambulance, but Punkin stopped her before she could make the call.

"Kim you can't call the cops because we don't know what he's been doing" "But Punkin I don't want to lose him."

"We not; just give me a few minutes and I can patch him up."

Punkin worked her magic and Kim went out to clean up the car, from where Quies' blood had done linked everywhere. As she cleaned the car she found the Carbon 15 and the AK in the trunk. She panicked because she realized Quies was in some deep shit. Kim found an old towel that she had in the trunk and wrapped both guns up then took them inside. As she sat the guns on the floor, Pun kin was just finishing patching Quies up.

She looked at Kim and asked her what was in the towel. Kim unrolled the guns and Punkin mouth dropped; she already knew what was going on. Punkin told Kim to help her lock all the doors and turn off all the lights. As they ran through the house Kim took a second to grab her 40 cal and met Punkin back in the living room.

"Aye Punkin do you know what's going on?" "Yea, Quies has been beefing with my ex-boyfriend"

"Bicth !! So you are the reason my baby is all shot up."

"He is not all shot up, it's only one shot and Quies and I was doing fine before you came in the picture."

"The way I feel right now I don't care about you or that baby. My man is laying up here with a bullet in him because of you."

Kim continued asking questions to see how she could help the situation even tho she was pissed. As time went by Kim and Punkin got sleepy, they ended up falling to sleep on the love seat. 12:30pm Quies woke up hungry as hell, looking around he noticed that he was back at Kim's house. Seeing Punkin and Kim sleep, made him wonder how he made it all the way back from East Atlanta. Quies got off the sofa and went to the kitchen.

As he searched the refrigerator he found a piece of chicken and one cube steak.He was so hungry he did care what he ate, he just wanted something to eat. Walking to the microwave Quies took a bite of the chicken, then sat it back on the plate inside the microwave. As he heated up his food he checked out his womb. The sound of the microwave going off woke Kim and Punkin.

They came in the kitchen screaming from the excitement that he was up and feeling better. Quies was startled from the screaming he turned around and asked them what the hell wrong with yall. They didn't pay him no mind, they both ran over and started hugging and kissing all on him. He grabbed his plate and the hot sauce, then went back to the living room. As he sat down he asked Kim and Punkin would one of them fix him something to drink.

Quies grabbed the remote and turned on the T.V. Flipping through the channels to catch the news to see if anything was begin said. He caught channel 2 news talking about its coming up next after commercial break. He flipped it to Fox 5 and it was just coming on. Quies told Punkin and Kim to quiet down so he could hear he turned up the volume. "Fox 5 here reporting live from a crime scene or just a terrible accident. Firemen say that it came from gas but there was no sign of a leak. And it's hard to tell because everything has burned down. Wait! Wait! This just in, police are saying that they just found assault rifles under some burnt wood."

"Damn, I should have taken all of them damn guns", Quies said out loud as he was locked in on the TV.

"We have someone here from the neighborhood, Sir could you tell me what you know about the fire?"

"Well I can't tell you much, all I know is that there were a lot of gunshots, then out of nowhere we heard a big boom."

"Sir, when you say we, who are you referring too?"

"My wife and I were asleep but obviously we woke up ASAP."

"Ok Sir, thank you for your time and information."

"Well folks there you have it, it's a crime scene, and if anyone knows anything please contact the local police department. Wait this just in, they say they found a finger or a toe belonging to Patrick Walkman. Stay tuned for more information when we come back from commercial."

Quies dropped his head and began crying. He knew if they found anything that would lead them to him it would be over. Kim took running up stairs; making it to the room, she grabbed her safe and the extra money she had hidden in the floorboard. Then she ran back downstairs and told Quies and Punkin to come on, they had to get out of town. Punkin grabbed her pocketbook and Quies grabbed the shirt that was on the couch and they all hit the door.

Quies headed for the BMW, but Kim told him they were taking the Infiniti G35. As they hit the road, Quies asked where they were headed. But Kim didn't know for sure because she had stomping grounds all over the US. Kims plan was to get as far from Atlanta as possible. Then it hit her as she was driving down the expressway, Colorado.

Her mom and dad owned some property up there that had a lot of land. They could hide up there and be safe for a while. Kim looked over at Quies and told them they were headed to Castle Rock (Larkspur), Colorado. Quies made himself comfortable so he could enjoy the ride.

Next stop Colorado to be continued.

MAINTENANCE MAN 2

CHAPTER ONE

"Wake up yall we are here" Quies opened his eyes and slowly rose up, to read a sign that readied Fuller Town and County Properties. As they drove down the road, he didn't see nothing but trees and every now and then a road that sat off to the side. He looked at Kim and asked her where the hell she had him at. Kim smiled and told him that they were in Castle Rock, Colorado. Kim finally reached her driveway, she couldn't stop smiling.

It's been years since she has been home. Pulling up to the house, Quies looked around and noticed that he was surrounded by trees. He liked that because he knew it would be hard for anybody to find him out there. Kim parked the car and everyone got out. As they walked inside the house Kim told them to make themselves at home.

Quies and Punkin walked around the house to give themselves a tour. They couldn't believe how big this was. Quies begin to wonder what her parents did for a living, and what made Kim move to Atlanta. Because she had everything she needed or ever wanted. Quies walked around the house until he found Kim.

She was seating in the theater that was built into the house. She was on the phone crying, so he sat down next to her and waited until she got off. Soon as she put the phone down Quies asked her who was that and what was wrong. Kim told him that her parents were mad at her for being pregnant and not married. Quies took her by the hand and told her not to worry about it, because they were married in their own little way.

He grabbed Kim and told her to let him make her feel better. She started smiling as Quies began kissing on her. Kim loved Quies because he always made her feel better no matter what. Quies got on his knees and pulled Kim's pants off, and started kissing all on her kitty. She lends back in the seat and lifted her legs up and puts them on his shoulder.

Quies began playing inside of Kim with his tongue and sucking on her clit. The more he sucked and played, he felt himself getting hard. He unfastens his pants with one hand as he continues using the other one on Kim. Then he slowly pulls up and grabs Kim by her hips and moves her closer. Then grips his dick and places it inside of her.

Taking one good stroke and Punkin came running in the room. "Quies come quick you gotta see the news" He looked at Punkin and asked her if she was serious as he took a few more strokes. Then he got up and ran back to the living room, to see on CNN NEWS they were talking about what he had done. Quies had to take a seat cause he didn't know his crime scene would make the world news. He couldn't stop shaking his head.

He knew it would be a while before he could go home .But the only good thing was that they didn't say if they had a lead. Quies was pretty sure that he didn't leave any evidence behind. CNN went from talking about his case on to the killing in Baltimore. And how the protesters weren't lying down.

The world is getting tired of the law killing people and getting away with it. Quies turned off the T.V. and sat back on the sofa. Kim and Punkin didn't know that Quies had done all of that, but they sat down next to him and told him that it would be ok. Instantly Quies brain went to working. He knew that he had to take care of Punkin and Kim.

But he didn't know his way around Colorado, so that was a good and a bad thing for him. Then it hit him, he could become a pimp. He saw how he had Punkin and Kim all over him and it didn't take long. Then he thought about which one he was going to pimp, was it gone be Kim or Punkin. The more he thought about it the more he realized that it couldn't be either.

He had to find some new chicks. And what better way to get a hoe, then to use a hoe. Quies sat up and told Kim and Punkin to listen to his plan to survive in Colorado. They weren't going for it at first until Quies put his foot down. Kim and Punkin looked at each other then said ok daddy with a smile on their face.

Quies knew that this was gone work out just fine. Ready to put his pimping to work, he grabbed the car keys and went for the front door. Punkin stopped him and told him that it was too late to be out there today. He looked at the clock and it was 9:45 pm. Quies turned to Punkin and told her that it was good timing.

"Baby just think about Paradise Maintenance Service. How Shun was running it." "You right baby we need to plan it out more."

"Ok then we will work on it all day tomorrow, but for now me and Kim got something planned for you."

Punkin took Quies by his hand and took him to the master bedroom. He was looking for Kim but she wasn't in the bed. Then he heard her call his name from the bathroom. Punkin took Quies to the bathroom where Kim was sitting in the hot tub. Quies took off his clothes and jumped in the hot tub.

Punkin took her clothes off and slowly walked over and started dancing for them, as she worked her way into the hot tub. Kim and Punkin begin kisses on Quies. Kim took her hand and started massaging his dick until it got rock hard. Then she sat on his lap and grinded her way upon a nut then got up and let Punkin have her turn. Quies wasn't focused at all, all he could think about was making his money.

He stood up and bent Punkin over and started stroking her fast to catch his nut. Quies smacked Punkin on the ass then got out the tub. As he walked to the bed he noticed that Kim was already asleep. He climbed in bed next to her and laid there, until Punkin got in the bed. She laid her head on his chest while he wrapped his arms around them and fell asleep.

Printed in the United States
by Baker & Taylor Publisher Services